The Way of the Gun

Fired from the Provost ranch and humiliated in front of the whole bunkhouse, Duke Latham swears vengeance on the owner Maynard Provost. Pursuing a life of crime and violence at the head of a small gang of outlaws, six months later Latham kidnaps Provost's beloved daughter Dulcie.

Provost's ranch hands scour the country searching for the girl, but in vain. Then fate throws them, and Provost himself, into the path of notorious bounty hunter Wesley Sumner, known as 'Certainty' because of his countrywide reputation for never failing to find and kill his man. Sumner is persuaded by the desperate father to take up the search for Duke Latham and his kidnapped prisoner.

The Way of the Gun

Ralph Hayes

A Black Horse Western

ROBERT HALE

© Ralph Hayes 2018
First published in Great Britain 2018

ISBN 978-0-7198-2663-4

The Crowood Press
The Stable Block
Crowood Lane
Ramsbury
Marlborough
Wiltshire SN8 2HR

www.bhwesterns.com

Robert Hale is an imprint
of The Crowood Press

Typeset by
Derek Doyle & Associates, Shaw Heath
Printed and bound in Great Britain by
CPI Group (UK) Ltd, Croydon, CR0 4YY

ONE

It was just under six months since Duke Latham had been fired from the Provost ranch, and he had already taken up the lawless ways he had succumbed to before his employment there as Maynard Provost's foreman. He had gathered three men around him of like disposition, and they had already robbed two business establishments at gunpoint, and held up a stagecoach on a local run.

His first year at the Provost ranch had gone well for Latham. Provost had known nothing of Latham's outlaw past, and Latham seemed to have a way with the cowboys who tended Provost's cattle. But then a couple of shady deals with cattle buyers, and Latham's inappropriate flirting with Provost's sixteen-year-old daughter had upset Provost once too often, and he had dismissed Latham in front of the whole bunkhouse, humiliating Latham and causing him to make a silent vow to serve Provost with a deserved 'payback' if the opportunity arose.

Now, on a cool day in late April, he and his new partners in crime sat around an abandoned trapper's cabin discussing their immediate future. Latham and two of the others sat at a crude, weathered table, while the fourth stood against a nearby wall. The man at the wall spoke to Latham in a gravelly voice.

'You want to hit that stage again, Duke?' They had made a nice haul from the first robbery. 'We could hit them on a different run. Maybe when they got some gold aboard.'

On a low-slung gunbelt hanging on his right hip he wore a wicked-looking Joslyn .44 revolver, with which he had murdered his own cousin at a very early age. He was Luis 'The Leper' Saucedo, as he had had a mild case of leprosy in his teenage days, which had burned itself out. He still had a badly scarred forehead from a botched surgery, and an egg-sized lump on his neck that he tried to hide with a soiled neckerchief.

'We can't hit them again right now,' a cohort at the table responded. 'It's too soon, they'll have guns on board now.' He was tapering up a cigarette from a tobacco bag, not looking at the others. The law knew him as One Ear Weeks, and he had already killed a half-dozen men in his dark career, a couple of them lawmen. He was considered the fastest draw of the small group, and he was always ready to use the Wells Fargo revolver on his hip. But he would never challenge Latham. His left ear was completely gone, the result of a knife fight, leaving a grotesque scar in its place.

The other cohort at the table, a brawny, broad-coupled fellow, was Ira Sloan; Latham had ridden with

6

Sloan in his pre-Provost days, and he was Latham's right-hand man because he was smarter than the others. A Schofield .45 hung menacingly on his left hip, because he was a southpaw. He had won prizes for shooting when he was a young man.

'Duke has some ideas about what's next,' he said in a gruff voice. 'Why don't you let him do the talking?'

Duke Latham took a deep breath in. He was in his late thirties, and athletically built, and some women considered him handsome in a rather dark way. He was taller than the other three, and there was an unnerving look in his eyes that made others uneasy in his presence. Nobody had ever taken him down in a gunfight, and it would not have occurred to any of the other three to challenge him. He had once made Bill Longley back down with the Starr .44 he wore low on his left hip. He was also a southpaw.

He was slouched into the back of his chair now, his demeanour giving him a rakish look as he mulled over the remarks of his subordinates.

'Actually, I've been giving some consideration to a sweet little bank I just run into over in Blaneyville when I rode over there yesterday for that Colombian coffee I like.'

'A bank?' Saucedo said, frowning from his position against the wall. 'Are we ready for that, Duke? They got these new-fangled safes they're using now.' He touched his bandanna to make sure it was covering the egg of flesh on his neck, and the thick scar on his forehead glistened dully in the light from a nearby window.

'What do you know about banks, Lumpy?' Weeks

laughed in his throat.

Saucedo's ugly face darkened, and he started to reply.

'Hold it down, you two,' Sloan growled, 'and listen.'

'I'll have to pay it a second visit,' Latham went on, as if the others hadn't spoken. 'But the safe hasn't been replaced. It must be fifty years old. Anyway, a safe is only as strong as its weakest officer staring into the muzzle of my gun.'

Ira Sloan grinned. 'Well said, Duke.'

'I like the idea,' One Ear Weeks announced, casting a smug look at the leper.

'We can ride back over there together, you and me,' Sloan suggested to Latham. 'I'd like to see that safe, too. Compare it with others I've done.'

'Good idea,' Latham told him. Despite his casual manner in that room, everything on Latham was spit-and-polish. The Starr on his hip looked like it had just come off a factory assembly line. He wore it in a custom cut-away holster that was always well oiled. 'I want you to look the people over, too. And look for alarms.'

'Why aren't we going?' Weeks asked with a frown, referring to himself and Saucedo.

'You don't have to know anything,' Latham said irritably. 'Just remember which end of those guns to point.'

Weeks looked hurt, but Saucedo just grunted in his throat.

'Incidentally,' Latham went on, rising up on his chair and sitting forward. The others watched every movement, hung on every word. He was the undisputed boss. 'I have a little something planned for us before we go back to work.'

8

Even big husky Sloan narrowed his eyes quizzically. 'What do you mean, Duke?'

'This isn't for money,' Latham went on. 'This is for payback to Provost.'

'That rancher that fired you?' Saucedo frowned. 'Are we going to start rustling cattle now in our spare time?' He gave a low giggle.

Latham's whole demeanour changed, and he spoke to Saucedo in an easy, even tone. 'If you make one more comment about things you know nothing about, you misshapen fleabrain, I'll blow your liver out past your backbone.'

A lead-heavy silence fell into the room like a swamp fog, and everyone there was reminded why they gave such deference to the man in the dark clothing with the dark countenance.

'I was just funning, Duke,' returned Saucedo, almost inaudibly.

Latham turned to Sloan. 'That bastard boned me, Ira – in front of the whole damn bunch. I can't just move on and act like it never happened. Provost needs a lesson in life.'

'You going to take him out?' Sloan wondered.

Latham shook his head. 'He has a small army to defend him out there. And they probably suspect I'll do something. No, that could get some of us killed.' He took a deep breath in. 'I'm taking Dulcie.'

'Who's Dulcie?' Weeks said.

Ira Sloan was frowning heavily. 'Provost's daughter?'

Latham gave him a crooked smile. 'That little brat bad-mouthed me to Provost more than once. I'd still be

9

out there except for that little high-and-mighty. I've got it all worked out. I'm taking her from him.'

'You mean kidnap her for ransom?' Weeks suggested. 'How much would Provost pay?'

'I told you, this isn't for money,' Latham said, staring across the room, his lean face sombre. 'I'm taking her permanent. Provost will never see his spoiled brat again.'

Sloan was sober faced. 'She's only sixteen, ain't she, Duke? What do you expect to do with her?'

'I don't want to shoot a kid!' Saucedo muttered. 'I'm superstitious about it.'

Latham glanced darkly at him. 'I don't want to kill her, you half-wit.'

Weeks' face changed: 'Oh.'

Latham looked over at him but said nothing. Ira Sloan still looked sombre. 'Do you mean, she would be with us?'

'She wouldn't be in the way. She can cook for us and keep our place clean. And whatever else I decide she should do.' He grinned. 'When you get a look at her, I don't think you'll mind having her around.'

Sloan shook his head, though. 'You'll have the whole damn county down on us, Duke. How can we operate under those conditions?'

'I'm way ahead of you, partner. After we take that little bank nearby, I've got big plans for us. I'm going where Provost will never find me, a world away from Ogallala and the Provost ranch. I'm heading for the Indian Territory. I hear the pickings are good down there.'

10

'The Indian Territory?' One Ear Weeks frowned. 'That's half way across the world!'

'That's just the way I want it,' Latham told him. 'Anybody don't want to go, you're free to go your own way.'

There was silence in the room. 'She takes a morning ride three times a week,' Latham went on, rather to himself. 'Across the ranch to the Wolf Creek crossing. She sometimes has a cup of coffee there, in the shade of some cottonwoods. She always has a ranch hand with her, but that should be no problem. I don't want him hurt. I want him to ride back and tell Provost what happened.'

More heavy silence. Finally, by Weeks: 'Sounds like a walk in the park.'

'We won't return to the cabin. We'll ride south. I might stop in Sioux Corners briefly to look for a guy named Quinn. He was fired from the ranch a while back, too, and might want to ride with us.'

Weeks looked over at him. 'Uriah Quinn?'

Latham nodded. 'He held up the Ogallala State Bank a while back. He's a good man.'

'He's dead,' Weeks said.

Latham stared hard at him. 'What?'

'I just heard it in town. Some bounty hunter gunned him down. Name of Sumner. Probably shot him in the back.'

'Good God,' Latham muttered.

'That would be Certainty Sumner,' Ira Sloan offered. 'Got quite a reputation. Never takes a man in alive.'

'Goddam swamp scum!' Saucedo blurted out.

11

Latham sighed. 'I was kind of counting on Quinn. If I didn't have this other thing going, I'd make the time to find this Sumner and introduce him to six feet of dirt.'

'I'd guess,' Sloan said, 'that where we're going you'll never see the likes of him.'

Latham made a sound in his throat. 'Well. Let's get back to the Provosts,' he said quietly. 'That's what our business is.'

'When are we going?' Sloan asked him.

Latham regarded him impassively. 'Why, tomorrow morning, Ira. It's Dulcie Provost's day out.'

The next day was a bright, cool one. Dulcie Provost was up just after dawn, and went out to the stables to prepare her pinto stallion for a morning ride on Provost property. After that she came back into the sprawling ranch house and had coffee on a rear patio with her father.

As they sat across a small round table from each other, enjoying the fresh prairie air briefly before Dulcie headed out, Maynard Provost found himself staring at his daughter.

'You know, I haven't noticed lately, but you're turning into a grown woman right before my eyes, young lady. Your mother would have been proud of you.'

Dulcie gave him a big smile. She was just barely sixteen, but her body was already very adult, and Provost had some trouble keeping the ranch hands away from her. She was a pretty girl, with big, green eyes and thick auburn hair, which was now caught up behind her head

12

so she could accommodate it to the small-size Stetson she wore on her rides. Because of being brought up by her father after her mother's early death, she had learned to repair barbed wire, drove cattle, and occasionally break a bronco. But she was very feminine, in both looks and manner.

'I miss Mother every day,' she finally responded to him.

'She would have made you into a lady,' he said with a smile. He was a tall, thin man with silver in his hair and a lean, lined face that was weathered from riding the cattle trails. 'I don't know how to do that.'

'You're doing just fine, Papa,' Dulcie smiled at him.

His face sobered. 'You keep away from the help, honey. You're too young for serious stuff with men. That's why I fired that Latham. I'll horsewhip any of these men that molest you.'

'I can take care of myself, Papa,' she assured him. 'Anyway, I like a little attention now and then. Practically speaking, I'm a grown woman, you know.' She rose from her chair. 'I'm heading out, Papa. I'm taking Corey Ross with me today. It's his turn.' A knowing smile. 'I'll be back way before you want to eat. I'm going to make you a surprise.'

'You're a good daughter, honey. Enjoy the morning.'

Fifteen minutes later Dulcie had found young Corey Ross, boarded her favourite pinto stallion, and was on her way for a sunny spring outing. Ross was one of the younger cowpokes who nursed a secret crush on Dulcie despite her youth. It was a two-hour ride out to Wolf Creek, which was the south edge of the big Provost ranch, and where Dulcie often spread a cloth on the ground and enjoyed a second cup of coffee with her chaperone before returning home. They didn't talk much on the way there. The cowboys who took her out had learned that Dulcie liked silence on her rides.

They arrived at the Wolf Creek ford at mid-morning, and were letting their mounts drink at the small stream when four men rode out from the cover of young cottonwoods downstream a short distance.

Dulcie and Ross turned in surprise at their approach, and Dulcie recognized Duke Latham immediately. She wheeled her pinto around, frowning. She had never liked him during his tenure at the ranch.

'What are you doing out here, Duke?' she demanded in a hostile tone. She looked the other three over warily. 'Papa won't want you on his property.'

'Dulcie girl!' Latham grinned at her. 'Just as sassy as ever, I see!'

Corey Ross walked his mount up beside Dulcie's. 'You ain't supposed to be here, Duke. Maynard likes you even less than before. He heard some things.'

The grin slid off Latham's dark-visaged countenance. 'You learn how to tie your shoe laces yet, boy?'

Ross' face coloured slightly. 'I recommend you take your mounts across the Wolf before you get into trouble,' he blurted out.

'Never mind, Corey,' Dulcie said. 'This place is spoiled now. We'll just leave.'

But Luis the Leper had moved his mount up close to hers. 'Not so fast, girlie,' he said in his guttural voice. 'We ain't even got acquainted yet.'

14

She looked him over, and his appearance frightened her. But she responded boldly: 'You'd scare crows out of a cornfield,' she told him. 'Now get out of my way.'

But now Weeks had reined up beside her, grinning at her. 'I like this one, Duke. She's a little honey badger.'

Now Latham was facing her on his chestnut stallion. 'The thing is, Provost's daughter, you're not heading home this morning. Or ever.'

'Hey, now wait a minute here!' Ross exclaimed. His hand went out to draw his gun.

'I wouldn't do that, Corey,' Latham said easily. All three of his men had rested their hands on their weapons. 'I'd like you to live through this if possible.'

Ross slid his gun back into its holster.

Dulcie was very scared now. 'What do you think you're doing, Duke?' she said breathlessly. 'Papa will skin you alive if you hurt me!'

Latham grinned easily. 'I won't ever see your daddy again. And neither will you.'

Dulcie's mouth went dry. 'What are you saying, you trail bum?' she shouted into his face.

'I'm saying you spoke your last words to Provost when you last saw him.'

Dulcie's face blanched. 'You animal! You think I'd go off with you? I'm going home! Come on, Corey.' She started to wheel the pinto around, but suddenly Saucedo was there, grabbing her reins.

She took a short riding crop from her saddle, and began flailing at Saucedo with it. He threw his arms up in defence, but one blow got through and struck the thick scar on his forehead. He sucked in his breath, his

15

eyes became wild-looking, and he slapped Dulcie hard across her face.

Everything stopped in that moment, Corey Ross sucked his breath in, and his hand went to his holster briefly.

'Nobody puts a whip to me!' Saucedo was muttering angrily. Dulcie was crying quietly. Latham casually drew his Starr .44, aimed it at Saucedo's chest, and fired. Saucedo was punched backwards off his mount and hit the ground near Dulcie, kicking up dust there. He was dead when he hit the ground.

Dulcie let out a scream in the midst of her tears. Ira Sloan, still sitting off from the others, frowned and shook his head slowly.

'Jesus!' Corey Ross whispered.

Weeks just stared at Latham.

'Oh God!' Dulcie murmured through her tears. Her bravado was gone.

'I told all of you,' Duke Latham said in a hard, quiet voice. 'Nobody touches this girl but me.'

'What the hell,' Weeks muttered.

'Somebody might have heard that shot,' Sloan said to Latham. 'We'd better make tracks.'

Latham went to Dulcie himself, dismounted, and tied her hands securely to her saddle pommel. Then he handed her reins over to Sloan. Dulcie's cheeks were wet, but she couldn't dry them with her hands tied.

'Why are you doing this?' she said to Latham.

Latham grunted. 'Your daddy will figure it out. . .' He went to his horse and mounted up again. 'He's about to lose the thing most important to him. And he won't ever get it back again. Take a good look around, girl. It will be the last time you see the Provost ranch.'

'Please. Don't do this,' Dulcie pleaded.

'And you,' Latham turned to address Ross. 'I'm letting you ride back to tell Provost what happened here. I want him to know who did it. Say I hope he has a good photograph of his daughter. You know, to remember what she looks like.'

Then Latham and his two men led Dulcie's mount across the Wolf Creek ford and into her new, unexpected and dark future.

TWO

Close to a day's ride south of the Provost ranch, at about the same time that Duke Latham was absconding with Maynard Provost's daughter, a lone rider appeared in the back country town of Burley Crossroads.

He wore dark clothing and rode a black stallion, and he fairly bristled with guns. His primary weapon rested low on his right hip, a Colt .45 Peacemaker, the same revolver that Wyatt Earp and Doc Holliday were currently wearing, and snugged into a shoulder holster was a back-up one-shot Derringer. He also carried a Winchester lever action 1866 repeating rifle in a saddle scabbard on his mount's irons, and on its other flank an American Arms eight-gauge, double-barrelled shotgun.

His name was Wesley Sumner, and he was a bounty hunter.

He rode slowly into Burley Crossroads now, looking around him. He was just over six feet tall, with dark hair and eyes, and rather handsome, aquiline features. He was athletically built, but slim. The darkness of his clothing was relieved by a blue kerchief at his neck, and a dark Stetson finished off his rather sombre look.

He walked his mount down a sunny, dusty street and reined in before a saloon called the Prairie Schooner. In a pocket of his riding coat was a 'wanted' dodger on a man named Billy Del Rio, a thief and murderer with three thousand on his head, and Sumner had evidence that he would find Del Rio hiding from the law in this backwater village. Sumner dismounted and wound his reins over a short hitching post, then casually slid the Colt in and out of its holster a couple of times, hoping this was the end of his hunt for this man.

Sumner had no intention of taking Del Rio into custody. He restricted his hunting to those wanted dead or alive, and he had never brought a man in. That was why many lawmen and outlaws alike had begun calling him 'Certainty' Sumner. Of course, he never knew when a man he confronted would be lightning fast with his gun, or something might occur to make things go wrong. But he kept taking the risk because it was the only occupation he knew.

Sumner climbed three steps to the swinging doors and stepped into the saloon. It wasn't a busy afternoon there, but several cowboys were bellied up at the long bar, and there were a couple of tables of drinkers. An out-of-tune piano was making tinny music at the rear, and men were talking and joking at the bar.

Sumner's eyes narrowed down on a table not far away with two men playing poker at it, and nursing a bottle of Planters Rye. The man facing Sumner was Billy Del Rio, and his eyes squinted down on Sumner warily now, wondering who he was. Del Rio was a swarthy, blocky man

19

with a badly broken nose and hard, glittery eyes. He was wanted for three murders in the mid-west, and had already raped a teenage girl since his arrival here two days ago. Sitting with him was another outlaw known simply as Raven, a very thin fellow with a hook nose and very black hair, whose bony face wore a perpetual scowl.

Sumner took a seat at a table near the doors, and faced the two men. A waiter came, and he ordered a black ale. The music still played, and nobody had paid much attention to his entrance. His ale came and Sumner quaffed most of its contents, assessing the looks and actions of his prey at the other table, appraising the way he moved and noting the personality he displayed. Del Rio had lost interest in him now, and had gone back to playing cards with his new partner.

Sumner swigged the rest of the ale, and was ready to make his play. He was glad to have settled into the room without notice. But then circumstances intervened. Two cowboys moved past him, on their way out, and the first one stopped beside Sumner's table as he was about to get Del Rio's attention.

'Hey, looky here! Ain't you Certainty Sumner?' The second cowpoke had stopped with his friend.

Sumner muttered an obscenity. Over at the other table, Billy Del Rio laid his cards down and slowly turned toward Sumner.

'Why don't you move it along?' Sumner growled at them. 'You must have a cow to punch out there somewhere.'

But the cowboy wasn't paying attention. 'By Jesus! You're the man who killed Curly Quentin! You worked for Clay Allison!'

The second cowpoke's eyes were big. 'You're Certainty Sumner? My God, they say you're as fast as Wyatt Earp!'

Sumner finally looked up at them. 'I guess you boys would like to live past this afternoon.' The grins slid off their faces.

'Then I suggest you move your freight out of here while I'm still in a fairly good mood.' He had left his riding coat on his mount, and with his dark jacket pulled back as it was now, the big Peacemaker stood out menacingly on his hip.

The first cowpoke swallowed hard. 'Sorry, Sumner. You just get on with what you're about.' Then he and his companion hurried out.

'Holy Jesus,' the bartender muttered.

Billy Del Rio and Raven were both staring hard at Sumner.

'So you're Certainty Sumner,' Del Rio called over to him in a Spanish-accented tone. 'What the hell are you doing in this one-horse dung heap of a town?'

'I came here to collect the reward on you, Billy,' Sumner said in his easy, well modulated voice. 'You've graduated into the big time.'

'I've heard about you,' Del Rio said with a hard grin. The music had stopped, and a heavy silence filled the close confines of the room. 'I heard you're a back-shooting weasel that murders men for money.'

'I've heard that, too,' Sumner grunted – it was often a man's very last words.

'I hear Clay Allison taught you real good,' Del Rio

21

continued, playing for time, doing the same kind of assessment Sumner had engaged in earlier.

'I know where to oil the Colt,' Sumner said with a half-smile. He scraped his chair away from the table, rose, and moved carefully away from that obstacle.

Del Rio stood up, too, and his cohort Raven followed suit, looking very confident. Unlike Del Rio, he didn't know Sumner's reputation.

'Let me take him,' he urged Del Rio quietly. He was very fast with the Colt Navy revolver on his hip, and had never been beaten. He was one-quarter Mescalero and had killed three lawmen in Montana. But seeing the svelte, lean look of Sumner standing there facing him, Del Rio wasn't as eager to test himself.

'So it's both of you,' Sumner said easily. Behind the bar, there was a tinkle of glass as the barkeep set a shot glass carefully down. 'Who are you, boy?' Sumner asked the black-haired Raven.

'The last man you'll ever lay eyes on,' Raven replied with a grin.

'You got a dodger on you?'

'What's that to you?'

'If you haven't, I suggest you bow out of this,' Sumner told him. 'You're of no value to me.'

Raven laughed. 'No value? Why, you goddam snake! Go for your iron!'

'Boys,' the nervous bartender called over to them. 'This boy here is Certainty Sumner. Why don't you take it outside?'

Everybody ignored him, and silence returned to the room. Del Rio put a hand on Raven's arm. 'Do you

22

really think you can beat both of us, back-shooter? While we're looking right at you? Neither of us has ever lost a draw-down. Tell you what. If you're only after money, why don't I throw a thousand at you and send you on your way? You can walk out of here with your skin.'

Raven shot a look at him. 'Are you crazy? I'll take this scum by myself if you don't want him!'

Del Rio shrugged. 'You heard him, Sumner. Sorry.' A brittle grin. Then suddenly he drew his Colt .45 at the same moment Raven went for his revolver. Their Colts roared out almost simultaneously, making the overhead rafters shake with the explosions.

Sumner, though, had read Del Rio's eyes, and by the time the lead came flying at him, the long Peacemaker had magically appeared in his hand as if it had already been there, and from a crouching position he fanned the hammer of the big gun. He was hit in the collar of his shirt, and along his floating ribs as he sent lead in their direction. His first shot struck Del Rio in the high chest, and the second smashed into his cohort's sternum and exploded his heart like a paper bag. Then Del Rio was hit just under the right eye, and Raven in the throat. The back of Del Rio's skull blew away, sending blood and matter flying as he danced backwards across the floor, taking two tables down with him. Raven hit the floor a half-moment later, clutching at his throat with a bewildered look on his Indian face. His leg kicked the floor once, and he joined his partner in death.

Gunsmoke was thick in the room as silence settled

back in. Sumner twirled the Colt over twice in his hand and let it settle back into its holster. A nearby drinker uttered a low whistle.

'I tried to tell them,' the bartender muttered.

Sumner walked over to the bar, drawing a paper out of his pocket. 'Here. You saw the whole thing. It was self-defence. Sign this affidavit for the local authorities.'

The barkeep nodded. 'Anything you say.'

A middle-aged patron came over to Sumner. 'Excuse me, mister. That piece of cow dung you just killed raped my little girl last night, and he was coming back again this evening, and there was nothing I could do to stop him. You just did me and this town a big favour. I'll never forget it.'

Certainty Sumner stuffed the signed paper back into his pocket. He touched his side and crimson came away on his hand. 'No need for gratitude,' he said diffidently. 'Without the bounty I wouldn't have bothered.'

Then he left the saloon with everybody staring after him. Silent.

At the Provost ranch, everything was in a turmoil. Maynard Provost was in the large, carpeted parlour of his ranch house, pacing the floor, anger clouding his lean face. Corey Ross, the cowboy who had had to bring Provost the bad news about Dulcie, stood beside a gut-tered-out fireplace, watching Provost anxiously. Sitting on a long sofa, his hands clasped on his knees, his posture giving the impression he was about to begin a foot race, was Jake Cahill, Provost's trail boss and foreman. He was a thick-set, broad-coupled man with a weathered face from years on the cattle trail. He had taken over the duties of Duke Latham when Latham was fired.

Provost stopped pacing in front of Cahill. 'I don't understand it. How could you lose their trail? Do you understand how hard that makes it now? We'll have to scour this territory for them. Maybe even go outside it. And even then.' He was churning inside. Dulcie was the love of his life.

Ross spoke up for Cahill. 'They got on to a main trail, Mr Provost. Their tracks got all merged up with lots of others.'

'After that, we were just guessing,' Cahill said quietly. Provost had been impossible to talk to since his daughter was taken. 'We think they were headed west.'

'He came here from Montana,' Provost said to himself. 'We'll scour this territory from border to border. Then we'll head west if we have to.' He stopped pacing again. 'Do you two really understand? Every day that passes could place her in more and more danger.' He shook his head. 'God knows what that animal could be doing to her as we speak.'

'Don't think like that, Maynard,' Cahill said soberly. 'It's you he wants to hurt, not Dulcie. And he's already done that.'

Provost turned suddenly to Ross. 'And you! I ought to fire you, goddam it! You just turned my girl over to that bastard without firing a shot!'

Ross' mouth went old-paper dry. 'I'm real sorry, boss. But l told you. There was four guns on me. And if they'd killed me, you'd never have known what happened to her out there.'

Provost gave him a scouring look. 'I'm putting this on you, Ross. And you, too, Jake. I want you to take a couple boys with you, and get out there and find my daughter. I don't care where you have to go, or what I have to spend to get it done. I want my daughter back.'

'I'm sure we'll find her eventually,' Ross offered quietly.

Provost turned on him again. 'Eventually? What the hell is wrong with you, Ross? Is "eventually" good enough for you? We have no idea what this sub-human has in mind! I find out now that he's a thief and a murderer! Is he thinking of killing my girl? Using her for rape? Is he beating her while we stand here talking about it? Time is of the essence, damn it! I want you two out there before dawn tomorrow. And I want to be wired daily about your progress.'

Cahill rose to his feet. 'We'll begin by looking west of here. I'll check every saloon and hotel from here to Laramie if we have to.'

Provost went and stood nose to nose with him. 'And when you find Latham. . . .'

'Yes?'

'I don't want him and his men arrested.'

Cahill met his stony look. 'You want them dead.'

'That's right,' Provost told him.

'That will be my pleasure,' Cahill assured him.

The next morning, in the pre-dawn darkness, Cahill, Ross and two other ranch hands rode off to look for Provost's daughter. They inquired in several towns closer to the ranch that first day, including Ogallala, but

26

without any result. Then Cahill decided to head west, which he and Provost thought was the most likely direction. For days they rode in and out of big and small towns, inquiring at saloons, hotels and stores. They also talked to the local law in each place, in case Latham had broken the law as he passed through.

After almost a week, they came up empty-handed.

At the end of that time the four men stopped at a saloon in a small town called Lakota Wells. They were all dusty, tired and out of sorts. It was a clean-looking little town, on the western edge of Nebraska territory, almost into Wyoming. The four of them had stopped at the local city marshal's office and a rooming house and now the only saloon, known as the Trail's End. They entered in a group and took a table in the centre of the room.

It was a pleasant place, with a potted plant near the slatted doors, a scattering of sawdust on the floor, and a small Remington painting behind the bar, of Sioux Indians scalping a conestoga driver. A heavy bartender came to take their orders, and a moment later returned with a pitcher of beer with four glasses.

'You boys just passing through?' he asked, wiping his forehead with a bar towel.

'We're looking for a man,' Jake Cahill responded. 'Name of Latham. Duke Latham. Maybe you've heard of him.'

The other man's face changed. 'Maybe.'

'Has he been through here lately?' Corey Ross asked him anxiously.

The barkeep's eyes narrowed down. 'Why do you want to know?'

Cahill rose from his chair, and went around the table to the other man. He was a large, brawny man who was the best bronco buster Provost had. Without warning he threw a steel-hard fist into the barkeep's face. A bone snapped audibly in his cheek, and he went flying across the room and banged loudly up against the mahogany bar, then sliding to the floor in a sitting position.

'Sonofabitch!' the bartender muttered. He spat out a loose tooth.

'You'll push that saucy line too far, mister. Now, I'll ask again. Have you seen this boy Latham?'

'We ain't supposed to call the names of patrons,' the other man spoke past a thick mouth. 'It's saloon policy.'

'Well, this is Provost policy,' Cahill growled angrily. He turned to his three men. 'Boys, how would you like a little target practice to go with our beer?'

Ross and the other two lanky cowpokes gave him big grins, and they all drew their revolvers. In the next moment, the raucous roar of gunfire filled the room, as the four cowboys began shooting at house rules signs, kerosene lamps, gaslight chandeliers, and bottles on shelves behind the bar. Customers ran for the doors, and for cover.

'Jesus in heaven!' the bartender protested thickly. 'Stop!'

Cahill aimed his gun at the Remington painting. 'Maybe I'll rearrange the design of the picture, barkeep? What do you think?'

The bartender was gasping for breath. Patrons were cowering in corners. The cowboys had momentarily stopped, but gunsmoke was thick in the close air.

28

'No, don't!' The bartender was back on his feet, holding his hands out.

Cahill lowered the gun.

'He used to come into town. He raised hell here a lot. The authorities think he robbed a couple stagecoaches near here. That was three, maybe four years ago.'

'Four years ago!' Cahill yelled at him. 'Why the hell didn't you say so? Has he been in here lately? The last couple of weeks?'

The bartender shook his head vigorously. 'No, no. Nothing like that. Not recently.'

'You goddam lamebrain!' Cahill growled. He holstered his weapon. 'Come on, boys. We're done here.'

A few minutes later Cahill was at a local telegraph office sending Provost yet another wire with bad news. After that he joined the others at a small hotel where they had taken two rooms. He and Ross shared a room with two beds. They had just taken their guns off to relax before returning to the dining room for an evening meal, when a knock came at the door and it was the desk clerk.

'Sorry to bother you, sir. You have a wire from a Maynard Provost.'

When the fellow left, Cahill opened the telegram and read it to Ross.

'Got your wire. Stop. We need a palaver. Stop. Will be there in two days. Stop. Do not leave hotel. Stop. Maynard.'

'Oh, hell,' Corey Ross grumbled. 'Provost coming here?'

Cahill gave him a look. 'It's his daughter, Ross.'

29

'Well. At least if all the ideas are his he can't blame us when they fail.'

'I think he'll head through northern Wyoming into Montana,' Cahill conjectured. 'He knows that Latham spent a lot of time around Billings before he came to the ranch. We might just find her up that way.'

'He may drive us all the way to California,' Ross said heavily.

Cahill went over and stood close to Ross. 'If you think this is unpleasant, think of what that girl might be going through, damn it!' Cahill said loudly to him.

Ross looked sheepish. 'You're right. Don't pay me no mind.'

Cahill shook his head. 'You got clabber for brains, Ross. Shape up or I'll fire you myself. Now go get the boys and we'll go find that dining room.'

It was later that same evening when Duke Latham, his two men and Dulcie made hardship camp alongside a small stream in southern Kansas. They had purposely avoided riding through any town on the way south, since Latham wanted no contact with the rest of the world until they arrived in the Indian Territory.

They all dismounted under the shade of low cottonwood trees, and Latham, as usual, untied Dulcie from her saddle and helped her to the ground. She rubbed her wrists and glowered at Latham. 'I'm tired. When is this going to be over? Where are you taking me?' He had only spoken a few words to her on the entire trip.

'You're going where your daddy would never think to look,' Latham grinned at her. 'Weeks, get the horses watered and fed. Ira, maybe you can find some dry fire-wood nearby. Dulcie, as usual, you get the pans out and the food. You'll be fixing us some rabbit and beans. This ain't your daddy's ranch now, where you had a cook and a housekeeper. This is the real world, sweetheart. It's your world now. You might as well start getting used to it.'

'Do you know how much trouble you're causing your-self?' she asked him.

Latham laughed, and Weeks joined in over by the horses.

'The only one that could be in trouble is you, Provost offspring,' Latham explained harshly to her. His aquiline face was tired-looking now. This whole thing had been very emotional to him. 'You're mine now. You belong to me, just like as if I'd bought myself a new, fancy pair of brocaded boots, or a new mount.'

Weeks giggled as he came back from the gurgling stream: 'Just like a new horse!'

Ira Sloan dropped a small load of firewood on to the ground near Dulcie, sober-faced. He didn't like having a teenage girl to babysit. She was giving them trouble at every turn, and she was good to look at, young or not. She was all curves under the tight riding pants and shirt, and Weeks was already sneaking hungry looks at her.

'I got her pans out,' Sloan said to Latham. 'That will save her some trouble.'

Latham turned to him and said fiercely, 'I don't want you to save her trouble! If anybody saves this spoiled brat trouble, it will be me!'

Sloan eyed him soberly. 'Right.'

31

'I don't want the damn pans!' Dulcie fairly yelled at Latham. 'I'm through cooking and working for you low lifes! I'm not hungry. If you're hungry, cook your own meal!' She walked over and kicked one of the pans into the creek, and it floated away downstream.

Latham walked over to her casually, turned her around, and slugged her in the face. Dulcie gasped when his fist hit, and then went flying to the ground. She lay there unmoving, a low moan issuing from her throat.

Latham stood over her, eyes wild, his breath coming short. 'You goddam mini-Provost! I should put a bullet in your head! You don't know how good you've got it, girl. I could have shot you right there at Wolf Creek. That was my first notion, you know.'

'She can't hear you,' Sloan told him gravely, shaking his head slowly.

'She's out cold!' Weeks grinned, his scarred ear site glowing dully in the small fire Sloan had just started.

'She's coming around,' Sloan said.

Dulcie moaned again, and moved her head. Her eyes fluttered open. Weeks stood over her, running his eyes over her body, grinning. Dulcie saw Latham, and focused on him, her green eyes narrowed down.

'You . . . hit me.' Thickly.

Latham grunted, cooling off now. 'Welcome to your new world. Tie her hands and feet, Weeks. And if she gives you any back-talk, gag her.'

Weeks got a happy look on his face. 'It's done.'

Sloan gave Latham a narrow look, then went and got some food from the saddlebags, to do the cooking.

Weeks spent several minutes on Dulcie, and took every advantage to brush Dulcie's curves, with Latham distracted at the fire.

Less than a half-hour later, when they were putting down rabbit, beans and corn dodgers, Dulcie was still bound hand and foot, on the hard ground at the edge of camp. Her mouth was bruised and bleeding, and her jaw hurt. She hadn't thought Latham capable of that kind of physical violence, and she was still shocked, lying there. She thought how good her life was just a couple of days ago, sitting and having coffee with her father on that lovely morning. Now that could be gone forever, she realized, no matter how much optimism she tried to maintain. She had no idea where she was, and she suspected Maynard Provost wouldn't, either. She fell into a deep depression, lying there on the hard ground and feeling the hurt in her face that Latham had put there. One thing was clear in her head. If Latham began raping her, she would find a way to kill herself. It was the lesser of two evils.

The three men were gathered around a low fire now, and rabbit meat was slowly burning on a spit. A tin of beans sat right in the fire. Duke Latham looked different from the way he had in Nebraska. His dark hair hung into his eyes, and his lean face showed new lines of fatigue. He didn't seem as relaxed as he had been earlier, not so much in control. He was obviously still working out what he wanted to do with Dulcie. In some corner of his mind she was a surrogate for Provost's deserved punishment. But she also had value to him. The difficulty was in assessing how much. He had always considered her a very attractive girl, even when she was fourteen.

After a short time they were all eating, but the food didn't taste good to Latham. Weeks was wolfing his meal down as if it were his last. Ira Sloan, looking broad-coupled and blocky sitting there on his saddle, hadn't spoken a word since they sat down. Now he looked over at Latham sombrely.

'You haven't talked much about exactly where we're headed, Duke. I for one would like to have a better idea of where this trail is taking us.'

'Who cares?' Weeks grinned past his heavy mastication. 'I'm having a great time!'

Sloan gave him an acidic look.

Latham set his tin plate down beside him, with food left on it. 'I didn't want to go into details until I was sure in my head what was best for us.' He swigged a cup of coffee. 'About a year ago I spoke with a drifter in an Ogallala saloon. He had spent most of his life in the Territory. Some of it running from the law.'

He looked out into the night. Over on the ground not far away, Dulcie saw him glance towards her before he continued. Off in the dark somewhere, a coyote wailed into the blackness.

'This fellow passed on through town and I never saw him again. But in that talk we had, he told me about a little town in central Oklahoma not far from a couple of Indian reservations. Name of Pawnee Junction. Just a few dozen houses, a store and a saloon. Outside of town a half-mile is an old house that's been sitting empty for over a decade. He thought a man could hide out there till hell freezes over and nobody would ever find him.'

'It sounds perfect,' Weeks opined. He looked small, sitting close to Sloan.

'What if that house is occupied?' Sloan suggested. 'You talked to that drifter a year ago.'

'Who cares?' Weeks said blithely.

'Then we'll have to do an eviction,' Latham commented darkly. 'We'll make that our permanent headquarters. There must be plenty of banks and stage depots within a hundred miles. I hear it's like a candy store down there.'

'Did you say permanent?' Sloan said.

Latham looked over at him. 'You said you wanted to make some money. You can't carry water on both shoulders.'

'We never stayed anywhere permanent,' Sloan argued. 'Eventually the candy will run out.'

'Duke will have his own private supply of candy,' Weeks grinned, jerking a thumb at Dulcie.

Latham cast a hard look at him. 'Just remember whose candy she is,' he said ominously.

The grin on Weeks' face evaporated. 'Sure, Duke.'

Listening distractedly to the conversation, Dulcie moaned softly, over by herself.

'That won't fill our bellies when the food runs out,' Sloan grumbled.

Latham caught his eye. 'When I said permanent, I didn't necessarily mean Pawnee Junction. We could move a hundred miles south and start all over again. The whole Territory is full of possibilities.'

'What if we get tired of the Territory?' Sloan persisted.

Latham gave him an irritated look.

From Sloan again: 'I don't mean to throw mud on nobody's plans. But I didn't like the girl from the first. She can only be trouble, and make trouble. I say take your pleasure with her and then end it.'

'End it?' Latham asked.

'That's right. She is Provost's daughter, ain't she? She is the enemy?'

Dulcie had heard the exchange. 'Don't kill me!' she mumbled.

Latham looked over at her. 'Finishing it for her isn't in my head right now. Maybe it will be, I don't know. But for now I don't want to hear any more about it.'

Sloan shrugged. 'She's your property.'

'Yes. And don't either of you forget it.'

Sloan sighed inwardly. 'I'll untie her and give her some beans.'

Latham shook his head. 'No, you won't. She said she wasn't hungry. She won't eat till we get to Pawnee Junction.'

Over on the ground, Dulcie frowned at him.

So did Sloan. 'That could be two days,' he said slowly. 'Are you sure?'

'What do you think?' Latham replied, staring into the fire fiercely.

Sloan studied his dark countenance. 'Right,' he said, without inflection.

'Right, starve her!' Weeks grinned laconically from across the crackling fire.

36

THREE

Maynard Provost sat quietly staring into a beer mug. He was in the Last Chance Saloon in Billings. Montana, and it was a busy Saturday afternoon. Drinkers stood along the bar and sat nursing tall bottles at tables around the room. At Provost's table, sharing a pitcher of beer with him, were Jake Cahill and Corey Ross, looking glum. At a nearby table sat the other two ranch hands who had been helping search for Dulcie. The small group had made inquiries through Wyoming and eastern Montana before arriving in Billings, and had failed to develop any information about Latham anywhere. Provost had thought that if he led the mission they might have better luck.

That hadn't happened.

Provost ran a hand through his silver hair, and looked over at Cahill. 'Well. This is it. I don't know what to do next. He might have gone southwest. He could be in California.' He let a long sigh out. 'I may never see my daughter again, Jake. The hard truth is, that bastard might keep her from me for ever.'

'If that sonofabitch don't go to hell,' Corey Ross grated out, 'there ain't no use having one.'

'There's another couple of places we can check here in town,' Cahill reminded him. 'I don't know what to do after that.'

Provost slammed his fist down onto the table, making his men at the next table look up in alarm. 'Goddam it! It's so damn frustrating! I've always been her protector, Jake. Ever since she could crawl. And especially after she lost her mother. She expects me to make things right for her if she gets into trouble. Wherever she is, she's expecting me to ride in and rescue her. And here I am. Feeling completely impotent to help her. To wrest her from that evil man's grasp.'

Cahill sighed. 'Well. If she's not out here in Latham's old stomping ground, she's out there somewhere, Maynard. I'll keep at this as long as you want to.'

'Me, too,' Ross added.

Provost gave him a narrow look. He still hadn't forgiven him for giving Dulcie over to Latham, as illogical as that was. He turned back to Cahill. 'I appreciate that. But we could wander the country and come up with nothing, without some sliver of evidence to guide us. I hate to say it, but I think we have to return home. Regroup there. Double-check for any hints locally. I'm drained, Jake.'

Silence fell over the table, amid the clamour around them. A piano started up in a rear corner, and all the gaiety sounded bizarre to Provost's ears. He sat there thinking of all the good times he and Dulcie had shared over the years, and a tear welled up into his eye. Dulcie was his life.

'Maybe it is better,' Cahill agreed, 'to return to the

ranch. Hell, Latham might even have tried to get in touch with us. Maybe he changed his mind, and would give her back for a ransom.'

But Provost shook his head. 'No, that pond scum didn't do this for money. He wants to hurt me as much as he can. The longer he keeps my daughter, the more he gets back at me. He'll do this for as long as he's able.' His voice was sombre.

Just at that moment the slatted doors up front swung open, and Wesley Sumner pushed through them.

Nobody paid any attention to his entrance. The loud laughing and joking continued unabated, and the piano music was lively. Sumner, dressed all in black clothing, Peacemaker hanging ominously on his hip, stopped just inside the entrance and let his eyes sweep the room, examining each table and each drinker at the long bar. Only then did he walk over to the bar and order a double whiskey.

Over at Provost's table, Provost was telling Cahill that they would take rooms at a nearby hotel for the night, and leave for Nebraska early the following morning.

'The looking is over for now,' he was saying. 'I want to get back just as fast as our mounts will carry us.'

He went on about duties at the ranch, while Sumner, over at the bar, relaxed with his Red Top Rye. When the bartender came past again, he stopped him. 'Has a man named Jenkins been in here in the past few days?'

'I wouldn't know,' the other man replied. 'Is he a friend?'

Sumner swigged some whiskey. 'He's wanted by the law.'

The bartender's face sobered. 'Oh. You're one of them.' And he walked away.

Provost had taken no notice of Sumner. Drinkers laughed across the room, and the music played, and up front three more men entered the saloon. They were rough-looking characters, greasy drifters, and they bore a family resemblance. They wore soiled trousers and shirts, with various colours of vests over them. They came swaggering in arrogantly, and bellied up to the bar a short distance from Sumner, with nobody in between him and them. They all ordered ale, and then the bartender stopped across from Sumner again.

'Say, I know who you are. Looking for Jenkins. I heard you was in this area. You're Certainty Sumner, ain't you?'

'Go wash some glasses,' Sumner grunted at him.

But down the bar, the nearest drifter turned to stare at Sumner. He then leaned in to speak in low tones to the other two men drinking with him. Finally, he called down to Sumner.

'So we finally found you!' in a satisfied voice.

Several others at the bar turned to listen, and the saloon went quiet suddenly. Over at the Provost tables, all five men took notice of the new action. Sumner glanced down the bar.

'You are Sumner, ain't you?' the drifter persisted.

Sumner downed a swig of his whiskey. 'You writing a book or something?'

'I'm Jethro Walcott. You murdered my brother Jed almost a year ago. These boys is his other brothers.'

40

Now a complete silence had fallen over the saloon. At Provost's table, he and Cahill exchanged a look. Ross and the other two Provost men were caught up in the exchange at the bar, too.

'Your brother was a cold-blooded killer,' Sumner replied quietly. 'Now why don't you let it go?' He ordered another shot of rye.

'We been hoping to run onto you, back-shooter,' Jethro went on. He was the tallest of the three, and more dangerous-looking. All three were armed with sidearms, and seemed very confident with them. 'I reckon this is our lucky day.'

Sumner turned back to his drink. 'Why don't you do yourselves a favor, and let it go?' he said in a casual manner.

Jethro said something to his brothers, and they moved out away from the bar, fanning out into a half-circle. The barkeep, standing nearby, got a half-grin on his meaty face. 'Too bad, bounty man.' He had been washing a shot glass, and now held it motionless in his hand. 'They got you cornered.'

Sumner ignored him.

But now the threesome were all facing Sumner with their hands out over their weapons. They knew nothing about Sumner, and had heard only lies from associates of their dead brother. Because of their numbers, they had no fear of him at all.

'Turn and face us when you die,' Jethro barked out.

Somebody scraped a chair at the back of the room, and it sounded like a cannon went off.

At Provost's table, Jake Cahill turned to his boss.

41

'Should we try to stop this? That poor bastard is as good as dead.'

Provost shook his head. 'You can't stop it now, Jake. It will have to play out.'

Just at that moment, Sumner turned to openly face the three gunmen. 'Jethro, you're like a hog rooting in a bucket, looking for trouble you can't handle. Your brother was a stone killer that I shot in a simple draw-down. He deserves to be where I put him. If you want to go to war over that, it's your choice.'

A drinker down the bar was emptying a bottle of rum all by himself. He had moved away from the action. 'Kill him, boys! Put that money-for-murder bastard under six feet of good Montana dirt!'

That seemed to fire the brothers up even more. Their faces were flushed. Jethro's eyes were wild-glittery. 'Go for your iron!' Jethro gritted out.

A couple of men at nearby tables belatedly rose and moved off. The room was otherwise collectively holding its breath. Then the threesome began drawing, all at the same moment.

What happened next was hard to follow. By the time the first sidearm was in the hands of one of the brothers, Sumner's Colt appeared magically in his hand and began a raucous firing that assaulted the ears of all present. One by one the chunks of hot lead struck the gunhands of his adversaries as their weapons cleared leather, and one by one the brothers cried out in pain as their sidearms went flying and they grabbed their gunhands in violent pain. Then a fourth explosion from the long Colt and the drinker who had called out for

Sumner's demise saw his rum bottle shatter before his eyes, and send liquid and glass shards onto him. The Peacemaker then barked out a last time, and the shot glass the bartender was holding disintegrated in his hand without touching him.

All five shots had taken just six seconds. Gunsmoke hung thick in the air. Jethro was on the floor, holding his fractured hand and yelling. The other two brothers had staggered to the bar and were collapsed against it, holding their gunhands, both of which were shot. The drinker down the bar was looking at his shirt front with a curious expression, and the barman was staring at his empty fist where the glass had been. He turned slowly to regard Sumner in awe.

Sumner twirled the Peacemaker over three times backward in his hand, then twice forward until it settled smoothly into its well oiled holster.

Silence fell heavily back into the room, except for the moaning of Jethro Walcott. Provost and Cahill exchanged another, longer look.

'Sonofabitch,' somebody muttered from a dark corner.

The bartender and the liquor-splashed drinker were both eyeing Sumner warily. Sumner spoke to the former. 'Pour me a Planter's Rye. Then get them out of here.'

'Yes, sir.' In a muffled tone.

Now a buzz started around the room, as Sumner received his drink and took a swallow of it, as if nothing had happened. The bartender guided the three subdued brothers outside, and directed them to a

43

doctor down the street. The liquor-stained drinker followed them, making a wide circuit around Sumner.

By the time the barman returned, still eyeing Sumner cautiously, Sumner was finished with his drink. He threw a couple of coins on to the bar.

'Thanks for the hospitality,' he said acidly. He turned to leave, and found Jake Cahill beside him.

'Wait a minute, Sumner,' Cahill said. 'Mr Provost at that table over there would like to have a word with you, if you can spare the time.'

Sumner glanced over at Provost and Corey Ross. 'No,' he said. He started around Cahill.

'Please wait,' Cahill urged him.

Sumner stopped, and looked into his eyes. 'What's this all about?'

'Provost likes what he saw there. He's a rancher from Nebraska. He's out here on a quest.'

Sumner frowned. The room had returned to normal now. 'A quest? What the hell does that have to do with me?'

'Just let him buy you a drink,' Cahill said.

Sumner sighed. 'Oh, hell. I'll give you that long.'

They walked over there together. When Provost saw him up close, he physically felt the proximity of this dangerous man. His mere presence filled the immediate area with a feeling of impending violence.

Provost asked him to sit down, and he took a chair. Cahill sat near him. Sumner glanced diffidently at Ross as Provost called out an order for drinks all around.

'I'm pleasured to meet you, Sumner,' Provost told him. He introduced Ross. 'And those men at the next table are my people too. They work on my ranch in Nebraska.'

Sumner said nothing.

'From what we heard, you're a bounty hunter.'

Sumner's face fell into more sober lines. 'And I guess you'll have some thoughts about making a living that way. Is that what you brought me over here for?'

Provost shook his head. 'Not at all. I know all about the profession, and find no fault with it. I was particularly interested in the way you handled those three men. It was very impressive. You managed a bad situation well.'

The drinks came, and Sumner took a swig of his. 'Well, I don't often receive any compliments for what I do. I appreciate it, and the drink. When I'm finished with it I'll be on my way.'

'We're staying at that hotel across the street,' Provost went on. 'I was hoping you'd meet us there later for a serious talk.'

Sumner was frowning again. 'Talk? About what?'

'I might have some work for you.'

'I have work. And it keeps me pretty busy.'

'I know. But this could save a girl's life. And the pay would be substantial.'

Sumner absorbed that. 'It would have to be. I don't work a bounty under five thousand.'

'And you never take a man in alive,' Provost said with a half-smile.

'You hear a lot.'

'I finally remembered your name. We know about you, even in Nebraska. But I never knew how good you are. Till I saw what just happened in here.'

Sumner studied Provost's face, and decided he could trust it. 'I'm in the middle of something. A man named Jenkins. He was reported to be here in Billings, but he's gone. I can't just quit on him, and it could take a while now to track him down.'

'I hear you'll take six months to track a man down. That's the kind of man I need for this. Look, let's just talk some about it. But not here, with all this noise.'

Sumner studied his face some more. 'I'll give you a half-hour,' he finally told him. 'And I'm not making any promises.'

They all went to the hotel together, and Sumner reserved a room before he accompanied Provost and Cahill to a large suite on the second floor. They sat around the room in overstuffed chairs facing each other, with Provost's and Cahill's guns and holsters thrown on to the nearby bed. Sumner kept his on. He still wore the dark jacket over the shoulder holster bearing the one-shot Derringer, but neither of them even knew it existed, yet. He leaned back in his chair and removed his black Stetson, and placed it on his knee and Provost assessed what a handsome figure he presented. He did not look like a killer. Except when he was obliged to use the Peacemaker that still hung, ominous, on his gunbelt.

'Now,' he said. 'Your half-hour just started.'

That made Provost a bit anxious, and irritated. 'Mr Sumner. Have you ever heard of a man named Duke Latham?'

Sumner looked at the ceiling, thinking. 'When I first

started all this, somebody by that name held up a stage not far from here. And he might have broken the law in Wyoming, too. But there was never enough of a bounty on him to get my attention.'

Provost nodded. 'Well, I didn't know all that, and I hired him to work for me at my ranch. When I figured out he wasn't the kind of man for us, I fired him. He apparently went crazy about the firing, and a few weeks ago he abducted my sixteen-year-old daughter. There was no ransom demand. I think he intends to keep her.' He paused, and stared at the floor for a moment.

'He was always harassing Dulcie, at the ranch,' Cahill cut in during the pause.

'She's just an innocent kid, Sumner,' Provost went on. 'And God knows what he's doing with her, or intends to do. I'm hoping that if we find him, it won't be too late.'

'He sounds like a sonofabitch,' Sumner conceded.

'That's an understatement,' Cahill growled.

'We thought we'd find him out here, where he came from,' Provost went on. 'But we've come up empty-handed.'

'What makes you think I could find him?' Sumner said.

'You have the experience. At keeping after a man till you locate him. We're novices at this.' He caught Sumner's eye. 'We need you, Sumner. I need you. You might be my last chance to ever see her again.'

Sumner sat quietly again. Then, finally: 'I'd be out five thousand with Jenkins.'

'Latham has two men with him. I'll pay you five for each of them. And another ten for bringing Dulcie

47

home to me.'

Sumner narrowed his eyes on Provost. 'That's a lot of money.'

'That's how important she is to me. That would make up for Jenkins and quite a bit more. Of course, I'd want the three of them dead. But that shouldn't be a problem for you.'

'I wouldn't consider it under any other conditions,' Sumner told him.

Provost smiled at that. Sumner got up and walked over to a dark window, and the two other men watched him.

'I worked for Clay Allison for a short time on his ranch. That was after his day of the gun. I don't see how anyone could do that, year after year. Ranching.' He was still looking out the window.

Provost and Cahill exchanged a smile. 'I guess it has to be in a man's blood,' Provost offered. 'How did you come by your profession?'

Sumner didn't turn from the window. There was silence for a moment. 'A friend of mine was murdered. He was just a kid. He was beat to death by two federal marshals, down in the Territory. That was right ater I'd gotten out of a hellhole of a Texas state prison.'

Provost and Cahill exchanged another look, but a sombre one. Sumner turned back from the window.

'I went after the two marshals and killed both of them, but by that time they were both on the wrong side of the law themselves.' He paused. 'After that, I just kept on going after killers.'

Provost studied that lean face. 'I guess I have to ask this. What got you thrown into prison?'

Sumner caught his eye. 'Murder.'

Provost furrowed his brow. 'I see.'

'When I was just your daughter's age, and living with my aunt, three men came in one night and raped and murdered her. They beat me senseless and left me for dead. I later found them, one by one, and killed them. The law thought I ought to think about that behind bars for a few years.'

Provost blew his cheeks out. 'Sounds like you're a man that takes matters into his own hands. None of that bothers me, Sumner. Will you go get my daughter for me?'

Sumner resumed his seat in the chair. He took a deep breath in. 'I wouldn't tolerate any interference. And I wouldn't want any assistance. I work entirely alone.'

'Done,' Provost said, sitting forward on his chair.

'And I'm not a miracle worker. If you can't find her, I may not be able to.'

'I have great confidence in you, Sumner,' Provost told him.

Sumner made a sound in his throat. 'I won't take anything for your daughter, if I'm successful. You never know what shape she'll be in, anyway.'

'Well, I'd like to. . . .'

'Is there anything about Latham's background I should know?'

'He never talked much about his past,' Provost answered.

'I just remembered,' Cahill said. 'He talked to a drifter

49

once that was high on some town in the southwest. Texas
or the Territory. Latham was saying how excited this
drifter was about the place. When you mentioned the
Indian Territory I remembered. But this must have been
almost a year ago.'

'I never heard that,' Provost offered.

'I didn't think it was important,' Cahill responded.
'But hell. Maybe he went south or southwest, Maynard,
instead of west.'

'If I wanted to go where nobody would ever find me,'
Sumner said, 'I'd head for the Territory. That's where
everybody goes that's running from something.'

'Damn!' Provost muttered. 'We've been looking in
the wrong places.'

'Maybe,' Sumner mused. 'You could just have missed
him here in Montana. Or he could be in Canada.'

'But you'll start on this for me? Tomorrow?'

Sumner hesitated, then nodded. 'I won't want any
payment until I bring her home to you.' He rose and
settled the Stetson back on to his head. 'Where's the
ranch?'

'Not far outside Ogallala. Anybody there can direct
you out to the ranch.'

'There won't be any reporting. You won't hear from
me again until I show up with her or I give it up as a lost
cause.'

Provost and Cahill rose, too. Provost extended his
hand. 'I appreciate this, Sumner.'

Sumner took it, and Provost was surprised by the iron
in the grip. 'Don't thank me. I've done nothing. But
I'll put all my time and energy on it. I wish you

well, Provost.'

'God speed, Mr Sumner,' Provost replied soberly.

In a sleazy little saloon in Pawnee Junction, down in Indian Territory, One Ear Weeks sat at a table with another man whom he had just met, and they had been drinking heavily. Weeks was supposed to be watching Dulcie at the old house they had rented, a couple of miles from town, while Latham and Sloan were off to a neighbouring village, looking into robbery possibilities. But Weeks figured an hour away could cause no harm since there was no way, really, for Dulcie to run. He had intended to be back in an hour, but he had been there almost two.

The place was quiet early that afternoon, with just a few other patrons scattered about the beer-odorous room.

'Yeah, we got this place not far from town,' Weeks was saying in his high, and now slurred, voice. 'It works fine for a headquarters. And you ought to see what we got out there.'

The other fellow was a tall, stringy man with wrinkled clothing and straw-like hair, and was a drifter just passing through. He had bought most of the drinks. 'Yeah? You got a stash of rum out there? I ain't had none of that for a goddam year.'

'No, no. Something better than that. We got this sweet little filly out there. Stole her from up north. A hot tamale.'

'A girl?'

'Yes, a girl, pea-brain. Just a kid, but you ought to see

51

her. She makes a man's tongue hang out.' A conspiratorial grin.

His companion returned the grin. 'So. That's how you spend your time at night.'

The grin evaporated from Weeks' narrow face. 'Naw. We got this partner. He thinks she belongs to him. It's hands off for the rest of us. And even he ain't tasted that yet. It's a goddam waste. She's ripe as a low-hanging fruit.'

'That don't seem right.'

'Tell me about it.' He looked around himself conspiratorially. 'Listen. Buy the next round and I'll show her to you.'

'Really? Hell, yes. I'm in!'

Less than an hour later Weeks and his new friend arrived at the house.

It was a run-down Victorian place with the paint gone and a broken porch railing. Weeds grew up high around the yard, where Weeks and the other man, who called himself Seger, hitched their mounts to a short rail. They climbed up to the porch and Weeks unlocked the front door. Latham and Sloan were not due back until much later, and in Weeks' inebriated state he had no fear of entertaining his companion briefly before sending the fellow on his way.

When they stepped inside they were in a wide parlour cluttered with old, weathered furniture, including a long sofa that was losing its stuffing. There was an archway to a kitchen, from which Dulcie now emerged.

She was wearing a low-cut blouse and floor-length skirt that Latham had bought for her in town. Her auburn hair had fallen down on to the sides of her face from some work in the other room. She held a dish towel in one hand, and now brushed at her hair with the other.

'Oh. It's you,' she said quietly. 'You're lucky you got back before Duke.'

Seger took one look at Dulcie, and uttered a low whistle. 'Woo-ee! You wasn't lying to me, partner! She's a honey!'

Weeks' face showed the pride of showing off a prize possession. 'Ain't she something? Dulcie girl, this is my new friend Seger. He just wanted to meet you and jaw a little.'

'Duke won't like this,' she warned him. 'Now, please excuse me. He'll beat me if those dishes aren't washed.'

Seger walked over to her. 'No, wait, honey. Let me get a good look. We ain't hardly met.'

'I'm not interested in meeting you,' she told him in a hard voice. 'I recommend you leave while you can.'

Seger was leering at her cleavage. 'I have to admit. You got it all, honey. I'd like to see you with that shirt off.' A crooked grin. She could smell the liquor on his breath.

'Damn you, Weeks!' she said angrily. She turned to leave, but Seger caught her arm, making her drop the dishcloth. She gasped as he turned her to face him.

'We can talk a minute, can't we?' Seger said thickly, his breath coming a little short now.

Weeks suddenly looked sober. 'I . . . wouldn't do that, Seger,' he managed in an uncertain voice.

'We come out here to see her, didn't we?' Seger

argued. 'I'd like to see more of her!'

When Seger reached down to unbutton the top button of her blouse, several things happened very quickly. Dulcie yelled in protest, and then slapped him hard across his face. While Weeks began laughing at that, the front door opened and Duke Latham walked in.

Ira Sloan came in just behind him.

Latham stopped just inside the room and stared hard at the threesome over by the doorway to the kitchen. He had heard Dulcie yell.

'What the hell is going on here, Weeks?' he growled.

Weeks began sobering up fast. 'Oh. This here is a boy from town,' he offered with a tight grin. 'I just brought him out here for a taste of our up-north rye.' Lying quickly and easily.

Ira Sloan walked over to Weeks and, without warning, threw a fist into his face. Weeks went flying across the room, did a somersault over an overstuffed chair, and landed on his back against the far wall. He was stunned. Blood ran from his nose and mouth and he spat out a tooth as he tried to assess what had happened.

Latham went over to Seger, where he still stood next to Dulcie. 'What do you think you're up to?'

Latham's proximity was menacing to Seger. He, too, was sobering up fast. 'Why, we just come out here to meet up with the girl. Just to say hello, you know?' He swallowed hard. 'We didn't mean no harm, mister.'

Latham looked over at Dulcie. 'What did he do?'

Dulcie shook her head. 'Nothing. He didn't have time.'

'I wasn't going to do nothing,' Seger said quickly, glancing over to where Weeks was sitting up and wiping at his mouth.

'What the hell, Ira!' Weeks mumbled past a swelling mouth.

'I'll take your gun,' Latham said easily to Seger.

Seger's face showed new fear. 'Hey. Now wait a minute here!'

'Your gun,' Latham repeated.

'Let him go,' Dulcie said from a few feet away. 'He's drunk.'

'Shut up and get into the kitchen,' Latham said in a monotone. 'You know what will happen if that place don't shine in there.'

Dulcie looked from him to Seger, then obeyed orders and disappeared into the other room.

Latham held his hand out, and Seger reluctantly drew his revolver and turned it over to Latham. Latham gave it over to Sloan.

'You came out here for a little fun with the girl, didn't you?' Latham said then, in a calm, quiet voice.

'Oh, no! Like Weeks said, we was just going to top off our drinking here. Then I was leaving.'

Latham shook his head. 'Boy, you're brash as a fry cook doing brain surgery. Thinking you can come in here and take my woman.'

'He wasn't doing that!' Weeks cried out, getting weakly to his feet. 'I wouldn't let nobody touch Dulcie, Duke. You know that!'

'Get out of my sight before I shoot you,' Latham growled out. Weeks hesitated, then left the house.

55

'Well, I'll be on my way, too,' Seger said, dry-mouthed.

'You're not going anywhere,' Latham said. 'And you don't have any say-so in this. Understand?'

'I just want to go back to town,' Seger said weakly.

There was a table and chairs over at the end of the room, and now Latham pointed at them. 'Why don't you take a seat over there?'

'Look, mister. I don't want any trouble. To be honest, I'm just a drunk that don't know what he's up to half the time. I wouldn't never hurt your girl.'

Latham guided him to a straight chair and Seger reluctantly sat down. Latham joined him, and Ira Sloan seated himself comfortably in a soft chair near the sofa. Watching but not speaking. Neither man had drawn his gun.

Sloan began paring his nails with a penknife.

'How long have you known Weeks?' Latham asked pleasantly.

'Oh, we just met this afternoon,' Seger said quickly. 'It was his idea to come out here. I just come along because it was a slow afternoon.' He tried a grin. 'I'd never come if I was sober. I reckon I should have give up John Barleycorn years ago.'

'You just met at the saloon?' Latham said.

'That's right. I'd still be sitting there if he didn't invite me out here.'

'Did anybody else know where you were going?' Latham pursued.

'No, not a soul. It was just the two of us.' He searched Latham's face. 'Anyway, I'm real pleasured to meet up

56

with you boys, but I got things to do in town now.' He started to rise, but Latham stopped him.

'I'll tell you when you can get up.'

Seger sat back, looking more afraid now.

'You live in Pawnee Junction?' Latham continued.

Dulcie came to the doorway to the kitchen. 'Nothing happened, Duke. Just let him go.'

Sloan turned to her. 'Better keep out of it, girl.'

'One more word from you, and I'll have a session with you tonight,' Latham warned her in a brittle tone. He had already beaten her once at the house.

She disappeared back into the kitchen. Feeling responsible for Seger.

'You didn't answer me,' Latham then said to Seger.

'Huh? Oh, I'm just passing through. Look, mister. I ain't no danger to nobody. I'm just a boy that minds his own business, you know what I mean?'

Over in his chair, Sloan was shaking his head. Latham began rapping his fingers on the table in front of him. He looked up at Seger. 'I got no hard feelings for you, Seger. You can rest easy on that score.'

Something that had grabbed Seger's insides like a clammy hand now released its hold on him a little.

'I'm actually a little sorry you came out here,' Latham went on. 'Considering the situation it puts you in that's irreversible.'

Sloan let a quiet, grunting grin move his face. Seger turned quickly and stared at him then turned a puzzled look at Latham.

'Situation?' Seger managed.

Latham arched his brow. 'Why yes. It's pretty obvious

you can't leave here now. Whatever happened with the girl. It's our privacy, you see.'

Seger frowned heavily at him. 'Can't leave? But I have to leave.'

'It's too bad. You're just a clabber-for-brains nobody that don't deserve this. Would you like a cup of coffee? I'm sure Dulcie has a pot ready out there.'

Seger was beginning to understand. He tried to speak, but his tongue clicked on his mouth. 'No, thanks. But. About leaving.'

'I've often wondered,' Latham said, as if Seger had not spoken, 'if I was shot, where I would prefer it. You know, if it was a fatal shot. In the head, or right over the heart. Both would be fast, of course. But maybe the head shot would be a little faster for you. On the other hand, some men might have an objection to getting it in the face. What do you think, Seger? How would you like to receive that fatal shot?'

Seger couldn't speak now. He tried twice and failed.

'Just mention your preference to Ira, and he'll remember your choice,' Latham added. 'I'm going to have a cup of coffee. You sure you won't join me first?'

'Don't – do this,' Seger croaked out.

'Well, OK.' He rose. 'Now you can get up.' He turned to Sloan. 'Go find Weeks. After it's over, let him do the dirty work. There's a shovel in the shed.' He helped Seger to his feet. 'You go along with Ira. You and he and Weeks can talk about your afternoon at the saloon.'

'Please,' Seger said thickly.

'Go on now.'

Sloan took Seger by the arm, and Seger almost collapsed from his grasp. A moment later they left together, and a couple of minutes after that a shot rang out from behind the house.

In the kitchen, Dulcie jumped slightly, and a shiver passed through her. Then Latham was there, looking relaxed and casual. 'Now. What's on for supper, girl?'

FOUR

Sumner had been on the trail for several days. He was riding a route that he figured Latham would take as he was headed for the Oklahoma Territory. He had inquired at saloons, hotels and marshals' offices in Sioux Falls, Keamey and Wichita, but without any evidence that Latham had been in any of those places. Now he had ridden into Dodge City.

He had been there on other occasions. The last time there he had tracked down a serial killer who called himself The Mortician, and had killed him in a wild gunfight in a saloon there. The marshal L. C. Hartman didn't like him, and had ordered him not to come back. But Sumner paid no attention to the wishes of marshals or sheriffs. Many of them disliked bounty hunters as much as outlaws.

Sumner checked again at two hotels and three saloons without luck, and was beginning to wonder if he had been right in his assessment of Latham's destination. The last saloon he stopped at was the Long Branch, run by Luke Short who was a personal friend of

Wyatt Earp, and had helped Earp recently end the Dodge City War with reformers peaceably. Earp and Doc Holliday were now long gone. But Sumner had met Earp in that very saloon a few years ago.

After having a quick drink with Short at the bar that evening, and being told he had never seen or heard of Latham or his men, Sumner joined three drifters at a nearby table who were playing One-Eyed Jacks.

They were all strangers to him, and a rough-looking bunch. The tallest of them sitting directly across from Sumner eyed Sumner's neat black attire with obvious disdain, thinking Sumner was a New Orleans or Natchez gambler.

'You from around here?' he asked Sumner as he dealt the cards for the first time to Sumner.

'No,' Sumner responded absently, receiving his hand and fanning the cards out.

The other man grunted. His face was lean and bony, with a badly broken nose. He wore a soiled neckerchief and a crushed-in, weather-mauled Stetson over shaggy hair. Hearing Sumner's curt response, he turned and exchanged a look with the drifter on his left, who was a short, stocky man with rheumy eyes. The third fellow, on Sumner's left, didn't look like he was with the other two. He was fairly well dressed and had a round, pleasant face.

'Pleasured to meet you, mister. I didn't catch your name.' Adjusting his cards.

'I didn't pitch it,' Sumner responded.

The tall one was studying Sumner's face. The friendly one beside Sumner wasn't deterred yet by Sumner. 'I wouldn't ask where you're headed.'

Sumner laid his cards down and looked over at him. 'Do you really need to know that, to play a few hands of cards with me?'

Round Face was embarrassed, finally. 'Sorry, mister. I didn't mean to get crossways of nobody.'

Sumner's face softened. 'I don't have a destination, boy. I just ride the trail. Trying to survive. Now can we play cards?'

'Just keep your hands above the table, Fancy Dan.'

Grinning at his companion. They had ridden in together at noon, and were hoping to make some quick cash at Luke Short's card table.

Sumner ignored the jab. He just wanted to pass the time for an hour or two before he returned to his hotel down the street. Winning or losing meant almost nothing to him. The tall man put his ante in and there was small betting around the table, and the tall man won the pot.

'I'll bet that surprised you, didn't it, New Orleans?' A harsh grin at Sumner.

'Why should it surprise me?' Sumner said evenly.

'You know why,' the tall fellow replied.

Sumner gave him a sombre look. The man on Sumner's right, the stocky, rather pudgy fellow, dealt the cards and the hand was played out rather quickly, and Sumner won. He raked in the pot as the tall drifter watched sullenly. Now it was Sumner's turn to deal, and he saw the tall fellow watching him closely as he dealt. Another hand was played, and the tall man bet big, and Sumner showed three jacks and won again. As he started to rake in the pot, the tall man stopped him.

'Just leave it there, New Orleans.' His hand was out over the Remington Army .44 on his belt.

Sumner released his hold on the pot. 'Anything the matter?'

'I think you stacked the deck on your deal.'

Sumner grunted out a short laugh. 'I've never cheated at cards in my life. Frankly, I wouldn't be any good at it.'

'I say you cheated, and I say that pot stays there, and you leave while you still can.'

Sumner just shook his head. 'Look. I came over here to relax for a while, not get into a big hooraw with anybody.'

'I'll just bet you don't want trouble,' the drifter grinned harshly. 'You just thought you'd clean us out and walk out of here like nothing happened. Well, that don't work at our table, Dandy. Now, if you reach for that pot again, I'll blow your liver out past your backbone.'

The round-faced fellow looked tense. 'Mister, I didn't see this man do no cheating.' Tentatively.

'Just keep out of it,' the tall man growled at him.

'Yeah, keep out,' his stocky companion echoed.

The other tables around them had gone suddenly quiet. Sumner was becoming impatient with the whole situation. 'I don't think you ought to push that saucy line too far, String Bean. You're getting right into my craw.'

Meanwhile, Luke Short had come around the bar and was heading for their table. He hadn't heard any of the exchange. 'How are the cards running, boys?' He saw the scowl on the tall drifter's face, but paid no attention to it. Before anybody at the table could speak, he turned to Sumner. 'There's a man up at the bar says he has something that might interest you, Sumner. When you're through here?'

Both the tall man and his cohort looked quickly towards Short.

'What did you call him?' the tall fellow said slowly.

Short smiled. 'Oh, I thought you'd introduced yourselves. This here is Wesley Sumner. Sometimes known as Certainty Sumner. Because of what he does for a living.'

But Sumner was looking towards the bar and the man Short had gestured towards. 'Is that the man?'

'Yes, the one nursing the glass of rum.'

Now the tall card player was frowning hard towards Sumner, and then he caught Luke Short's eye. 'Wait a minute. Did you say this is Certainty Sumner?'

Short nodded. 'The same, gentlemen. The one and only.'

'Holy Mother,' the stocky man muttered, turning towards Sumner with an awed look.

'My God!' Round Face whispered, looking at Sumner as if he had never set eyes on him before.

The tall drifter brought his gunhand up to his face and slid it across his mouth. Still smiling, Short left to return to the bar. The drifter cleared his throat.

'You're Certainty Sumner?' In a hollow voice.

Sumner regarded him soberly. 'That's right.'

'Good God. Forget what I said, Sumner. I know you'd never cheat at cards. What the hell was I thinking?'

'You don't know what I'd do or not do,' Sumner responded, raking the pot in. He rose from his chair. 'But you're one lucky card player, mister. Luke Short just saved your life.'

Then, with the three men staring slack-jawed after him, Sumner walked over to the bar, the Peacemaker on his hip suddenly looking like a cannon to the men at the table.

Sumner came up beside a very thin, lean-faced cowboy wearing ranch clothes and riding chaps. Sumner ordered a drink and the cowpoke looked over at him. 'I heard you talking to Luke. Sorry. Didn't mean to steal no privacy. I guess you're after three men.'

Sumner received his drink from Short's bartender and threw a coin on to the bar. 'Yes. And a girl.'

The cowboy swigged a beer. 'I heard about you. You worked for Clay Allison for a while.'

Sumner didn't pick up the shot glass before him. 'Is that why you got me over here?'

'No, no. My boss knew Allison. Said after his wild days he become a Webster on cattle.' He grinned. 'But he was a hard case for a while there.'

Sumner picked up the shot glass and downed its contents. 'Well, if you'll excuse me.'

He started to leave, but the cowpoke stopped him. 'No, wait, Sumner. I got something that might be important to you.'

Sumner sighed. 'Then spit it out. I want my mount bedded down.'

The cowboy turned to face him. 'I reckon you ain't

had no luck asking about your three men here. Or else-where.'

'Your time is running out,' Sumner said curtly.

A quick nod. 'Well, yesterday I was out looking for quail, for the supper table. South and a little east of here. I stumbled on a camp site where some riders had made hardship camp for the night.'

Sumner's eyes narrowed down. 'Go on.'

'The camp was a few days old. But there was still the tracks of several horses in dried-up mud. It could have been four.'

Sumner's face settled into pensive lines. 'Are you pretty sure it could have been four?'

'Pretty sure. And that matches the number you're watching for. Right?'

Sumner responded abstractedly. 'Yes.'

'I figure your party to be avoiding towns altogether,' the other man went on smugly, 'and are camping out every night to get where they're going.'

Now Sumner's face softened. That idea had occurred to him, but he hadn't pursued it. 'That might be very helpful. I'm much obliged. Exactly where is this camp site?'

'Take the main trail south for a half-hour till you come to a tall cottonwood. Turn off the trail there to the east, and ride a short distance to a small stream. You should find it within a few hundred yards along that stream bank.'

Sumner nodded, and laid a double-eagle gold coin on the bar. 'Here. You earned it.'

After some weak objections the cowboy accepted the

reward, and Sumner was on his way out the door.

Outside he stood on the porch for a moment, assessing what had just transpired. It was dark now and he would find lodgings in Dodge for the night, then head out early tomorrow to find the camp site the cowboy had mentioned. He hadn't looked around him because of his musing on the new information. But then he heard the soft cocking of a sidearm behind him.

Sumner drew, whirled, and fell into a half-crouch in one fluid motion. And there was the tall drifter from the card table, revolver already out and aimed at Sumner's chest. But he didn't fire. Seeing the Colt levelled at him, he threw down.

Sumner hesitated. The man's companions were gone. He shook his head and dropped the Colt to his side. 'What the hell were you thinking?'

The tall drifter grinned, embarrassed. 'I got this crazy idea. To be the man that took down Certainty Sumner. Go ahead, shoot me. I deserve it.'

'Boy, you ought to sell that sidearm before it gets you killed,' Sumner growled. He re-holstered the Peacemaker, descended the steps and mounted his stallion.

'Good luck to you!' the drifter called out as Sumner rode off without looking back.

Sumner stayed in town that night, and early the next morning he went looking for the camp site reported to him by the cowboy at the Long Branch. He followed the directions given him closely and soon found himself alongside the stream described to him. Three hundred yards downstream he found it, but almost rode on past it. Then he was dismounted and standing over the burnt place in the ground where the fire had been.

He could still discern the hoofmarks in the hard ground where the riders had been, and he noted that one set of hoofprints was lighter than the others, and might mean a lighter horse and rider, which could be Dulcie.

But that was scant evidence. He scoured the surroundings for clues, but without success. He went and sat on a tree stump nearby, and thought the situation over. He still wasn't convinced this was their encampment.

But then his eye caught the edge of something that looked out of place in the area. He got up and walked over to a spot beside a young tree, and saw a tiny piece of cloth showing at the edge of some leaves. He picked it up and held it in his hand. It was a torn bit of gingham, a fragment of blue cloth, and Sumner now recalled Provost's description of Dulcie's attire when she was taken. She had been wearing a blue blouse and tan riding pants. Under foot he noticed a lot of the light hoofprints, and guessed that Dulcie had got her blouse pinched and torn by her saddlery, leaving a small hole in the blouse.

'I'll be damned,' he said softly. 'I'm on your trail, Miss Provost.'

His earlier conjecture had been right. Latham was purposely avoiding any towns he passed, so he couldn't be traced. That made him clever. And therefore dangerous.

He stuffed the little piece of cloth into a pocket,

mounted the black stallion, and rode on down the bank of the stream. His whole feeling about the hunt was different now. His chances of eventually finding Latham had jumped to a fairly high level. But that still didn't guarantee success. He had to get past Latham and his men. And of course at some point Latham could have just decided he didn't want to bother with Dulcie any more, and disposed of her.

Sumner followed the stream all morning until it turned off to the east, at which point he kept on south, heading for the Indian Territory border. He realized that that territory was very large, and that keeping on Latham's trail would depend on finding another camp site, or other evidence.

In mid-afternoon he came upon a lone man encamped under a mesquite tree. He reined in several hundred yards away, studying the scene, satisfying himself that he wasn't riding into an ambush. Then he rode on into the other man's camp.

The fellow had been squatting on a fallen limb from the tree when Sumner approached. Now he rose warily as Sumner entered his camp area. His mount was picketed to the tree. Its saddlebags looked full, and there was a dark case affixed to the blanket roll behind the saddle. He appeared to be a commercial traveller of some kind.

He studied Sumner closely. He wasn't carrying a sidearm. 'Afternoon, stranger. I was just having myself a cup of coffee. The real stuff. Can I offer you a cup?'

Sumner looked the camp over, and then dismounted. When the other man saw his general appearance, and the Peacemaker, he felt his mouth go a little dry.

Sumner nodded. 'I'll have a cup. It's been a long, dry ride.'

The other man relaxed some. He went to his low fire, retrieved a small coffee pot and poured Sumner a cup.

'I'm pleasured to meet up with you, stranger,' he grinned. He was heavy-set and pot-bellied, wearing dark clothing and a lariat tie. He took a swig of his own coffee. 'I'm R. C. Funk. I spread the word of the Lord all through the Territory and Kansas. Glory be to Jesus our Lord and Saviour, and blessed be those who follow and accept Him.'

Sumner took a long swig of the coffee. 'That's good coffee. So you're a Bible drummer?'

'Yes, sir. I do a little preaching, too, when the opportunity arises, in one of these Godless communities I pass through. May I ask your name, sir?'

He had just violated a hard rule of the trail, but Sumner excused him. 'The name is Sumner.'

It meant nothing to Funk. 'I'm glad to know you, Mr Sumner. I hope you won't judge me too forward, but have you been saved for resurrection, sir? Have you accepted Jesus Christ as your Saviour?'

'I don't take much to preaching, Mr Funk.'

Funk grinned at him. 'That sounds like a negative reply, Mr Sumner. I'd like to make you the proud owner of one of our gilt-edged, completely illustrated Bibles, sir. May I show you one from my case over there?'

Sumner sat down on the fallen log to finish the coffee, and Funk sat down beside him, awaiting an answer.

'I limit my reading to the Kansas City paper,' Sumner said. 'You've been riding up from the south?'

'Yes, sir. All the way through the Territory. Just crossed the border early today. Glad to be away from that land of iniquity. But listen. If I can't persuade you to be the proud owner of the Good Book, maybe you'd like to get down on your knees with me and pray to Holy God for salvation. We'll do it together, Mr Sumner. It will make you feel redemption inside you.'

Sumner was impatient, but smiled at that invitation. 'I think I'll leave the praying to those that hate seeing my face for the first time,' he responded quietly.

'What do you mean, sir?'

'It's a long story,' Sumner told him. 'Have you done much camping along the trail on your way north?'

'Almost exclusively,' Funk replied. 'I'm a poor man, Mr Sumner, who can't afford the recent costs of taking a bed at a decent hotel where you don't wake up with welts on you from critters of all sorts.'

'Did you notice any freshly abandoned camp sites on the trail?'

Funk thought about that for a moment. 'No, I can't say that I did. But my route takes me off the main trail to one direction or the other. To hit the small towns in my general path, you see. That's where the Bibles are sold. And I might get involved in a tent revival.'

Sumner was disappointed. He threw some coffee dregs on to the ground, set his cup on the log, and stood up. Funk found himself staring again at the Peacemaker. He rose, too. 'Well. I wish we could have done business. Of one kind or another,' he grinned at

Sumner, studying his face and wondering what kind of a man he had run into.

'May I ask your profession, Mr Sumner?'

He had violated a second rule of the trail. 'You're a very curious man, Funk,' Sumner remarked. 'Be careful it doesn't get you into trouble.'

Funk looked embarrassed. 'Sorry. It almost did a couple days ago. I asked the same question and a man pulled a gun on me. His companions enjoyed the moment very much.'

'There was more than one man?'

'Yes, sir. Three, to be exact.'

'Was that meeting out on the trail, like this?'

'Why, yes. Directly south of here, in the Territory.'

Sumner tensed slightly. 'I don't suppose there was a girl with them?'

'Why, now that you mention it, there was. She kept in the background and didn't speak a word.'

'Was she just a kid? Wearing a blue blouse and riding pants?'

Funk's face lit up. 'Why, you must know the girl?' The brightness faded. 'And the men.'

'No. I just know about them.'

'One of them had only one ear. A frightful-looking fellow. He asked if I knew how far it was to Pawnee Junction. Then the one who had drawn the gun gave him a very mean look. And they rode on.'

Sumner couldn't believe this good luck. He narrowed his blue eyes down on Funk. 'Are you quite certain he said Pawnee Junction?'

'Oh, yes. I remember because I had stopped in there

on my way north. It's barely a town, it's so small. Nobody could afford a Good Book. Yes, it was Pawnee Junction, all right.'

Something relaxed slightly inside Sumner. 'And how far is Pawnee Junction?'

'Oh, once you get into the Territory, it will be most of a two-days' ride. Might you be going there too?'

Sumner gave him an acid look, and withdrew a coin from a belt poke. 'Here. What you just told me is worth more than a Bible to me.'

Funk was surprised. 'Why, bless you, young man!'

Sumner went and mounted the stallion, which was waiting patiently for him. Then he turned back to the drummer. 'You asked my occupation. I kill other men for money.'

Funk stood there assimilating that, then a heavy frown worked itself on to his pudgy face. 'Why – good heavens!'

'Oh. And if there is such a place as heaven. ...'

'Yes?' Thickly.

'I'll probably be headed in the other direction.'

Then he rode off to the south, with Funk staring after him, slack-jawed.

FIVE

Dulcie was making her bed up when Latham walked in. She turned quickly towards him, gasping slightly. Her left eye was badly bruised, and her green eyes revealed her new fear of him, and her hatred.

'Go ahead,' he said pleasantly. 'Finish it up. I'll wait.'

Dulcie made no reply. She turned and pulled a corner of the bed cover up, and then straightened it. She then turned back to him as he walked over to the bed and examined it without speaking while Dulcie held her breath. He supervised and inspected every task given to her in the house, and if it wasn't to his liking, he usually punished her. The black eye had been her most recent punishment.

'Good job.' He turned to her and touched the bruise under her left eye. She flinched, but made no complaint or objection. She had learned not to. 'Yes. That's looking better. If you took more care and did things the way I tell you, you wouldn't have this to deal with.'

Dulcie had found out already that Latham was as obsessive about his surroundings being just as he wanted them as he was with his personal attire, which was always military neat and orderly. And he was treating Dulcie like a slave girl who displeased him at her personal risk. However, he had given her her own bedroom, forbidding anyone to enter it but her and himself – and strange as it seemed to both Sloan and Weeks, Latham had not touched her sexually in all the time he had had her. But Dulcie expected it at any moment, which added to the tension that was inside her, day and night.

Latham smiled at her. 'What would you like to fix us for supper? You have any ideas?'

'We have some ham left over. Or I could go outside and get us a chicken.'

'Why don't you surprise us?' he suggested.

'You might not like my choice. I'd rather you decided,' she said.

He frowned slightly. 'You refuse to surprise me? When I just told you it would please me?'

Renewed fear took hold of her pretty face. 'No. Of course not. I'll pick one of them. After you're gone.'

He had already told her that he and Sloan would be gone for part of the day, and would leave her again with Weeks. For her, it would be a kind of vacation from fear while he was gone, so she looked forward to it, however unpleasant it was to have the ugly Weeks watching over her. Actually, Dulcie had fairly well given up on her father ever finding her down there, and had acknowledged to herself that her life as she had known it was over. She had even contemplated suicide, but even that would be difficult to accomplish as a prisoner in this house.

'I'm not locking you in up here today,' Latham was telling her. 'I'm trusting you to have full roam of the house. If Weeks leaves again, I want you to tell me about it. Understand?'

She nodded. 'All right.' She was still upset about the cold-blooded way they had killed the man Weeks had brought to the house.

'In fact, if Weeks causes any trouble of any kind, I want it reported to me. I'm making it your responsibility. And that's even if he threatens you not to.'

She nodded, realizing that this put her temporarily higher in the pecking order, ironically, than Weeks. 'He'll be all right. He's afraid of you.'

'The little bastard better be. Ira and me will probably be back by five or six. I want supper ready and waiting for us.'

'That won't be a problem.'

'If it's not, the problem will be yours,' he said pointedly.

'I know.'

When he left a moment later and she heard the outside door slam after him, she felt a clammy hand release its hold on her insides.

Latham and Sloan were heading for Lone Butte, a town almost sixty miles south-west of Pawnee Junction, where a very small bank had been established under six months ago. They had ridden there when they had first arrived in Pawnee Junction, taken a cursory look at the primitive facility, and decided that two of them could take it with relative ease.

They arrived in Lone Butte at midday; the weather was warm and dry, and they had damp sweat bands and slightly flushed faces. They rode on to the town's wide, dusty street and reined in at the Trail of Tears saloon just down the street from the Territorial Bank. They looked around, noting that the street was almost empty of traffic.

'Backwater,' Latham commented.

'But that's just what we want,' Sloan commented.

They spurred their mounts on down the street, and dismounted right in front of the small bank. There was an OPEN sign on a front window. They climbed three steps to the entrance, looked around them to see if they were being observed, then pulled their neckerchiefs up to cover their faces.

'Let's do it,' Latham said.

A moment later they were inside the bank, guns drawn. There was a very narrow reception area in front of a row of teller windows. There were three windows, but only two tellers. Behind them were several desks, where two women and one middle-aged man sat. The tellers were both men.

When the two walked in masked with guns drawn, one of the tellers looked up and gasped.

'All right, folks! This is a hold-up!' Latham barked out. 'Everybody do just what we tell you, and nobody will get hurt.'

They both went around behind the tellers. Sloan stopped beside the nearest teller and Latham walked over to the middle-aged man at a long walnut desk. Off to the left was a free-standing safe that took up most of the wall.

'Are you the manager?' Latham said from behind the bandanna, his Starr .44 levelled at the man's head.

The fellow swallowed hard, and hesitated. 'No, sir. He's off for the day.'

'Well, can you get into that safe?'

'No, sir. Only the manager can open that safe.' He was a heavy-set fellow wearing a neat vest and sleeve garters. 'I'd like to help you, but I don't know the combination.'

Sloan shoved his Schofield up against the near teller's cheek. 'Is that the manager he's talking to?'

The teller's eyes widened. 'Uh . . . yes, sir.'

Latham scowled under the cover. 'You stupid ass. Get over there and open that damn safe!'

Now the manager looked terrified. 'Sorry. I had to try to save our deposits. I'll co-operate.'

Latham swung the barrel of the Starr against the manager's head, and connected above his left ear. The manager was almost knocked off his chair. Blood began running down the side of his face, and he was gasping raggedly.

'Maybe that will add some incentive,' Latham growled. 'Now get that safe opened.'

'Yes.' Thickly, staggering to the safe and twisting a combination knob there. In a moment the safe swung open.

Latham leaned down and looked in. There were several piles of paper money, and a bag of silver coins. There were also some bonds and legal papers, which Latham ignored. He took a bag from his coat and began stuffing the money into it.

But as that was happening the teller farthest from Sloan surreptitiously drew a Derringer over-and-under from his cash drawer, turned it on Sloan, and fired.

Everybody was surprised, including his partner at the other window. 'Josh!' that fellow cried out.

Sloan had been hit in the high chest, and his look of surprise was quickly turned into one of hot anger. The teller had now aimed the Derringer at Latham, and was ready to fire the other shot from the small gun. Sloan, though, raised his left hand with the Schofield in it and fired, beating the teller. The hot lead hit the fellow behind his left jaw and blew his right ear off, the roaring making one of the women at a desk scream. Sloan leaned heavily against the cash counter.

'Are you all right?' Latham called to him.

Sloan nodded. 'I'm OK.'

Latham closed his bag up and came past the manager. 'Your teller just shot my partner, you bastard.'

The manager was breathless. 'That's against bank policy, sir! I'm sorry!' Casting a glance at his dead teller.

'Well, this is for that, and for lying to me,' Latham growled. He drew the Starr again, aimed it at the manager's face, and fired. A blue hole appeared in the other man's forehead, and brain and blood sprayed out the back of his head.

Now the second female clerk screamed, and then fainted, falling off her chair to the floor. Latham went over to Sloan, who had holstered his gun. There was crimson staining his shirt up high on his right chest, just under his shoulder.

'I feel better already,' he said. 'I'm lucky it was my

right side. It won't hurt my shooting. Let's get the hell out of here.'

When they arrived outside, they pulled their face covers down, but then a man appeared from a store two doors down. He looked like a rancher. 'Hey! What are you boys up to?'

Latham swore under his breath, drew the Starr .44 again, and shot the fellow in mid-chest. He staggered backwards for a moment, looked down at the hole in his vest, then toppled to the ground.

'Let's ride,' Latham grated out.

Sloan had some difficulty mounting, but then they were riding out of town in a gallop, figuring to keep ahead of the local law.

It was two hours later, when they passed through a small village with a veterinarian doctor, that Latham stopped to look at Ira Sloan's wound. Sloan was looking very fatigued from the ride.

'That lead has to get dug out,' Latham told him. 'We're stopping at the vet down the street there.'

'Ain't that dangerous?'

'We have no choice.'

At the vet's place a few minutes later, the vet took Sloan into a back room that smelled rankly of swine and ammonia, and laid him on a table smeared with blood-stains.

'This looks like small calibre,' he told Sloan, with Latham watching. 'It won't be very deep. It should be no trouble.' He was short, slim, and red-headed.

He gave Sloan a swig of laudanum and dug the lead out easily. Then he applied a thick bandage to the site.

80

'There. You'll have full use of that arm within a week or so. Now, if you'll just give me your name and where this happened, I can make out a bill for you.'

Latham drew the Starr once more for the day. 'Didn't you know, Doc? It ain't courtesy to ask a man's name.'

The vet turned just in time to see the revolver aimed at him. 'No, wait! I understand! I won't. . . .'

'Nothing personal, Doc,' Latham said pleasantly, 'but this has to be kept private. I'm sure you understand.'

The gun roared in the close confines of the room, and the vet ended up on the floor beside his exam table with a hole in his chest and a terrified look still on his lifeless face.

Two hours later Latham and Sloan were back at their headquarters outside Pawnee Junction. Dulcie had their fried chicken ready for them.

Just a few hours after Sumner had met the Bible drummer on the trail, he crossed over into the Indian Territory. Now two days later, he would spend one more night in hardship camp before riding into Pawnee Junction. He expected to be there early the following day.

He found a place to stop in a cluster of mesquite trees, where a large flat butte loomed off to the west. The site looked as if it had been recently used by other persona, and he wondered if it had been Latham and his men. He looked around for any sign of their presence, but found nothing. It had been a long day and he was tired. He picketed the stallion to a sapling and gathered some dry wood for a fire. He was out of food now, and had done no hunting for game, so would have to content himself with a cup of coffee and half a soda biscuit. He got the fire going and returned to the horse to retrieve the coffee, when he heard the metallic clicking of a gun being cocked behind him.

He swore under his breath. His fatigue had made him careless. Now he heard the soft whinny of a horse from behind a nearby rock outcropping, just before the voice directly behind him.

'Don't turn. Don't breathe or you're a dead man. Get them in the air.'

Sumner hesitated, then obeyed, raising his hands. 'I have little to rob,' he said, staring straight ahead. He felt a hand slide his Colt from its holster, and a heavy weight sank into his chest. But he wasn't completely defenseless. He was wearing his dark riding jacket because of the cool air, and whenever he put that on, he added the one-shot Derringer to his belt at the back, in its special, break-away holster. There was no way, of course, that he could get to that now.

'OK. You can turn now.'

Sumner turned to see a bearded, rough-looking man holding a Remington Army revolver on him. Sumner's Peacemaker was tucked into his belt. Sumner remained calm and casual.

'Take what you want. But there isn't much.'

'Did I tell you to talk?' the intruder said harshly. 'You look like a gambler, mister. Gamblers always have money stashed somewhere. You got gold coin in them saddle-bags, or hid in your bedroll?'

'I'm not a gambler,' Sumner told him. 'You're

wasting your time with me.' He realized he was only being kept alive because he might lead the intruder to a cache of wealth. 'Well. I do have a few coins.'

The other man's face brightened. 'Of course you do! That's more like it, hot stuff. Where exactly is this cache?'

'It's not a cache,' Sumner said, stalling for time, and feeling the Derringer heavy at his mid-back. 'They're in a leather poke, and I'll have to take a look for it.' Without asking permission, he walked the few feet to his mount, and rummaged through the near saddle-bag.

'It's on the other side,' he announced. 'Just a minute.'

Again, before the other man could object, he walked around the stallion past its head. He touched its muzzle on his way past because it was feeling the excitement in the air.

Once over there, he reached into the other saddle-bag, and nodded. 'Here it is. I think there might be several double eagles in there, and some silver.' He showed the intruder a leather poke, and then threw it over to him, over the horse's back.

'That's more like it, Dandy.' He momentarily pulled the string on the poke to look inside, dropping the level of the revolver at the same time. He frowned. 'Hey. There ain't no gold in here.'

When he looked back up, he was staring into the muzzle of the Derringer, over the mount's back.

'Surprise!' Sumner said soberly.

'Jesus!'

'Drop the gun,' Sumner ordered him.

The bearded fellow hesitated. Then he threw the revolver on to the ground. 'Who the hell carries a Derringer as a back-up piece? Who are you, mister?'

'Turn your back to me.'

'Don't kill me. I'm just a poor out-of-work trail bum.' He turned to face away from Sumner.

Sumner came back around the horse and walked over to the would-be thief. He picked the American Army up from the ground and stuffed it into his belt. Then went around to face the other man. He pulled his Peacemaker from the fellow's belt, and holstered both it and the Derringer.

'You wondered who carries back-up iron. I'm Wesley Sumner, and it's how I travel. I also carry a Winchester repeater and an American Arms eight-gauge in saddle scabbards, as you can see. Sometimes I have a Dardick hidden in the bedroll. I like to be prepared for flea-brains like you.'

'Damn!' the fellow muttered. Then: 'Wait a minute – Sumner. Ain't I heard that name before?'

'You were going to kill me, weren't you? After you cleaned me out.'

'Oh, Jesus.' Quietly. 'Certainty Sumner. I heard about you when I was in Laramie a year ago.'

'Is that why you're down here, you maggot? Because you're running from something in Wyoming territory?'

'You put your gun away. Are you going to kill me?'

'Do you have a bounty on you?'

He shook his head violently. 'Hell, no. If you'll spare me, I can put you on to a couple of boys that do.'

'I'll bet.' Sumner grunted out. 'Take that big neckerchief off.'

'Huh?'

'You heard me. And get over against that mesquite.'

In the next few minutes Sumner had tied the drifter to the tree with his own bandanna and gunbelt.

'What do you want from me? You don't have to tie me up.'

'Consider yourself very lucky,' Sumner advised him. He went and kicked the fire out, which had already guttered low. Then he went over to his mount and cinched up a saddle strap.

'Hey. You're not leaving, are you?'

'I'd already decided to move on, before you pulled your little stunt. There's no wood to make a decent fire here, and no water. I'll spend most of the night on board the stallion. I don't seem to need much sleep lately.' He was talking more to himself than the tied-up man.

'Well, wait! You can't just ride off and leave me tied up here! Take me in to the nearest town and turn me over to the law. At least I'll survive a little time behind bars. You leave me here, I might never get free of this. Some varmint could come and chew my leg off. Or I could succumb to thirst, and the elements.'

Sumner let a half-smile touch his face. 'Too bad you didn't consider all that before you came in here. If you'd caught me in a bad mood, you'd be dead by now.'

'I get that. And I'm much obliged. But I got to look for my cousin. He disappeared from Pawnee Junction a few days ago and ain't been seen since.'

Sumner had been about to get on his mount. Now he

85

turned back to the other man. 'Pawnee Junction?'

'He was drinking with this other fellow at the local saloon. They say he was an odd-looking bird with one ear. After a while they left together and my cousin never come back. I figure he's up north of here in Suggsville, where there's an ex-girlfriend. That's where I was headed when I – saw you.'

Sumner frowned slightly. 'He was with a man with one ear?' Provost had given Sumner a brief description of the three men who had his daughter.

'That's what I was told. Do you know him?'

Sumner made a sound in his throat. 'Weeks,' he muttered. That confirmed it. They were there. He looked over at the tied-up thief. 'Uh, no. Never heard of him.'

He mounted his horse with the knowledge that an impending confrontation with Latham and his men was a certainty. It was just a matter of finding them when he got there.

'You see what I mean, though?' the other man pleaded. 'I got important business to take care of.'

Sumner wheeled the stallion to face the failed thief. 'You'll get free eventually. And when you do, a word of advice. Find another profession to pursue from here out. You're not very good at this.'

Then he rode off with the bound man staring after him.

At the house just outside Pawnee Junction, Duke Latham had gathered Ira Sloan and Weeks in the wide parlour with him. He was sitting in an armchair, and Weeks and Sloan were slouched on a long brown sofa.

On a small table between them sat a tall bottle of unopened rye whiskey. Dulcie was in an adjacent room putting on a dress that Latham had just bought for her.

'There was a lot of shooting that day,' Sloan was saying. 'I know it couldn't be avoided. But it will draw a lot of attention to that bank.'

'What's the difference?' Latham said. 'There's only a half-dozen federal marshals to cover this whole damn territory.'

'But you never know when one will ride by,' Weeks offered. He watched Latham's face to see how his comment was received. Latham was still irritated with him about bringing a man from town to the house, the fellow who was buried behind the barn.

Latham gave him a narrow look. 'If you're afraid of US marshals, Weeks, why don't you ride on down to Mexico? Nobody here will miss you.'

Weeks looked embarrassed. 'I'm just saying.'

'If a lawman ever shows up here,' Sloan offered, 'we'll shoot the sonofabitch and bury him beside your friend out back.' He grinned at Latham.

'How's that wound healing?' Latham asked him.

Sloan moved his right arm around. 'It's fine. In another week I won't even remember it happened.'

'Because I'm going to need you healthy in about that time,' Latham added.

They both studied his lean face.

'That's why I was gone yesterday. I found another bank.'

'Jesus,' Weeks muttered.

Sloan frowned. 'You're thinking of taking another

87

one so soon?'

'Now you're beginning to sound like Weeks,' Latham said soberly. 'Look. I don't plan to make this rat-hole our permanent residence. I figure on cleaning out everything available within a hundred miles and then eventually moving on. We'll talk about that later. But for now, I figure the sooner we get done what we came here for, the farther ahead of the law we'll stay.'

'So where is this second bank?' Sloan asked him.

'There's a little town west of here called Old Fort. Used to be a cavalry post. There's a real bank there, one that's been there a decade or more. It's twice the size of the one in Lone Butte, and holds pay for ranch hands' salary for miles around. The take on any Friday should be three or four times what we got the first time out.'

'Let me go this time!' Weeks cried out. 'You know how good I am with this Wells Fargo, Duke! I'm tired of being nursemaid to that kid in there! I'll make you glad you took me.'

'You're not as smart as Ira,' Latham said flatly. 'You're unpredictable. I never know what you'll do next.'

'No, no! I'll make you proud of me! Just give me a chance to show you this time. It will give Sloan some extra time to heal.'

'I don't need extra time,' Sloan grinned at him. He looked over at Latham. 'We might need a third gun if we do that bank, though. They might even have an armed guard. Maybe for just one time we could leave her alone here. Lock the doors. The windows are nailed shut. Even if she got out, where would she go? We'd find her before she got a mile away.'

Latham glanced at him. 'I don't think you understand her importance to me. It's not just that she's Provost's little girl. She's kind of grown on me. In fact. . . .'

But before he could finish, the door to the adjacent room opened, and Dulcie came into the room.

All three men turned – and just stared. She was wearing a frilly white dress that Latham had purchased in town. It was narrow-waisted with a flare at the hips, and it showed plenty of Dulcie's cleavage.

Suddenly she gave the appearance of a very mature, beautiful woman. Her auburn hair was down on her shoulders.

Her black eye was turning yellowish.

'Good Jesus!' Weeks whispered.

Sloan just sat there, staring, a frown of surprise on his square face.

'What do you think, boys?' Latham grinned. 'Don't she fill that dress out? I knew she'd do something special to it.'

Sloan's look of surprise turned to one of sombreness. He had looked at her as a kid until that moment, but a beautiful woman in the house was quite a different thing. A thing that could be a portent of bad luck, both for her, and for them.

'Now can I go take it off?' Dulcie said to Latham quietly.

He frowned. 'Hell, no. Come on out in the centre of the room, kitten. I want the boys to get a good look at you.'

'Let me go change,' she protested softly.

Latham frowned with impatience. 'Do you want me to start on you?'

Her mouth went a little dry. 'No.'

'Then you do what I tell you. Whenever I tell you, and whatever it is. Get to hell out here where we can see you.'

Sloan shot Latham a sombre look. He didn't like any of this. If it had been up to him he would have taken Dulcie out back and put a bullet in her head.

Dulcie reluctantly came to the middle of the room and stood there motionless.

'Now turn completely around,' Latham ordered her.

She hesitated, then turned a complete circle, showing herself off to them.

'I like it,' Latham grinned.

'Good Jesus!' Weeks repeated. 'You really got yourself something there, Duke.'

'You touch her,' Latham said pleasantly, 'and I'll fill your gullet with lead.'

Weeks looked suddenly sober. 'We all know who she belongs to, Duke. Ira and me would never touch her.'

'I'm not concerned about Ira,' Latham retorted. He looked back at beautiful Dulcie. 'You do me proud, kitten. Do you know why I bought you that dress?'

'You wanted to show me off,' she said without looking at him.

'Well, that, too. But don't you see how that dress might be used?'

'I don't want to guess.'

'Why, that's a wedding dress!' Latham grinned.

All three of the others turned to him with shock on

their faces.

'What the hell!' Sloan muttered.

'Good Jesus!' Weeks repeated again.

Dulcie was staring at Latham as if he must have gone mad. 'What are you saying, Duke?'

'Why, isn't it clear as cloud peaks under sheet lightning? I'm going to marry you, sweetheart!'

Dulcie's eyes widened and her cheeks began burning. 'Marry me? Marry me? Why, I wouldn't marry you if my life depended on it!'

The outburst had come out without her really knowing it was going to. But it was the real Dulcie expressing itself. Latham grew a deep frown, and rose from the chair. When he walked over to Dulcie she backed up a step and winced slightly.

'Your life does depend on it,' he growled at her. He grabbed her and pulled her curves tight against him. He hesitated a moment as the physical touching aroused him. Then he spoke to her in a hard, ominous voice. 'Get this into your head, Dulcie girl. You're mine now. You always will be. In a few days now, you'll be coming to my bed. Every night. And because your daddy would hate it, I'm going to make it all legitimate. And to make you understand that this is it: you won't ever be returning to Nebraska. You'll be with me wherever I go. My legal wife. I'm going to look up a justice of the peace in the next couple days, and you'll marry me wearing this dress.'

Dulcie struggled fiercely to get out of his grasp. He finally released her, but immediately slapped her across her face.

She gasped, and her eyes became damp.

'The next time you struggle to get away from me,' he grated out. 'I'll beat you till you can't stand.'

'Let me go change,' she blurted out, her voice breaking.

'Sure. And be careful of the dress. I want you to look like an ice-cream sundae when we do it.'

Dulcie turned and left the room, her cheek inflamed from the slap. Latham grinned at Sloan, then went and sat down on his chair again. 'Is she something? It's like finding a sack of double eagles. I like it. I get my payback to Provost, and this for a bonus.'

'You got yourself something there,' Weeks said more quietly.

Sloan took a deep breath in. 'Duke, are you sure this is what you want?'

Latham frowned slightly. 'Wouldn't you?'

'I'm happy to satisfy my needs with a saloon girl now and then,' Sloan replied. 'You have your little party, you put your pants back on, you leave. And you don't have to be bothered with them till the next time.'

'So?' Latham responded.

'So you're carving out something very different for yourself. You're not the husband type, Duke. You've never tied yourself to any one woman. She'll be here twenty-four hours a day. When you get up, when you eat, when you want some privacy with us. If we move on from here, we have to cart her along with us. And she's a sweet little piece, I admit that. But she's the enemy, Duke. She's Provost's daughter. She will never have any affection for you. She may try to murder you in your sleep. She might try to murder all of us. You'll be sleeping with the enemy.'

Latham sighed. 'Don't you see? That's what I like about it. The spice that gives it. She's a feisty little bitch, and I like that. There will be bedtime like I've never had before.'

Sloan grunted. 'She makes the rest of us hungry, and that's not good. Look at Weeks. His tongue is hanging out for her.'

'Hey!' Weeks protested. 'I've seen you look at her, too.'

'That's just the point,' Sloan said. 'That can cause trouble. Among us.' He looked over at Latham, and spoke carefully. 'You seem just a little obsessed with her, Duke.'

Latham fixed a brittle look on him. 'I never get obsessed on anything, Ira, and don't you forget that. I'll keep her around as long as she behaves herself. And I won't brook any opposition to my having her. Unless you think you'd like to take over this little outfit of ours.' In a menacing tone.

'Of course not,' Sloan said quietly.

'Then I don't want to hear about it again,' Latham added. 'Now. Are we finished with this?'

'Absolutely,' Weeks spoke up quickly.

Sloan let out a deep breath. 'Whatever you say, Duke.'

Latham gave them a tight smile. 'Then let's talk about that Old Fort bank some more,' he told them.

SIX

As he had recounted to Marshal Provost on their first meeting, it had been a series of fortuitous occurrences that had led Wesley Sumner into hunting other men for the rewards on them. When he had emerged from a Texas prison in his early twenties, he had befriended a young man with a lovely sister who liked Sumner on first sight, despite his background. When Sumner and the new friend had gone looking for work in the Territory, they had been falsely arrested by federal marshals, who beat Sumner's friend to death. After his release for lack of evidence before a hanging judge, Sumner had vowed to visit justice on the marshals himself. And he did, when they turned lawless themselves, and they each had bounties on their heads, and Sumner had been persuaded to accept the money even though that had not been his motive. Then he returned to the sister, expecting to marry her and help her run her farm – but by that time she had already married. With a vacuous future confronting him, and no real training in any occupation, he happened upon a wanted poster on a building

94

wall, studied it for a long while, then stuffed it into a pocket. And he had begun a new career, one that seemed to fit his acquired skill with his Peacemaker. With the hatred inside him for all killers because of what had happened to his friend, he took his first sought bounty and never looked back.

Now, on that warm afternoon the day following the wedding dress incident at Latham's headquarters, Sumner rode into Pawnee Junction with an earned reputation in his chosen line of work.

As he rode slowly down the dusty street, he looked around with distaste. He had bad feelings about this whole area, because of his early experience there. That had been south of here, in open, arid country, and then at Fort Sill. But this had the feel of the Territory, despite its small size. Hot. Dry. Primitive. No law anywhere in sight.

He rode slowly down the only street. A saloon, a store, and a scattering of houses along a desolate stretch of so-called civilization. The only reason any man would come to such a place from elsewhere was, Sumner knew, because it was the end of the world. Safe from the law, and justice.

Sumner reined in at the saloon and dismounted. The building fronts looked dusty and unkempt. He walked down the street a short distance to the store, and went in. A tall, lean clerk stood behind a counter. There were stacks of canned goods and textiles on shelves around the room. Under the counter in a display case were arranged several kinds of sidearm.

The clerk looked Sumner over carefully. 'New in

town, stranger?'

Sumner gave him a look. 'Do you have a box of .45 cartridges back there somewhere?'

The clerk eyed the Colt on Sumner's hip. 'Sure, I can fix you up, mister. Would that be for your Peacemaker?'

'Just get the cartridges,' Sumner told him.

'Just making conversation, mister. We don't get much chance at it here in Pawnee Junction. I just sold three boxes of .45s to another man yesterday. But he wanted them for a Schofield.'

Sumner took notice. That was not a usual gun used in backwoods areas. 'What did this man look like?'

'Oh, he was a stout, tough-looking fellow. Had a scar under his right eye, and wore his gun on his left hip. Paid in small silver. Probably holds to his cash like the cholera to a Kiowa.'

'Sloan,' Sumner said to himself.

'Oh. I hope he ain't your friend. I was just palavering.'

'The cartridges,' Sumner said flatly.

When the clerk returned and Sumner had paid for the ammunition, he spoke to the man again. 'This fellow yesterday. Do you know if he's living hereabouts?'

'No idea. But he wasn't just passing through. I saw him walk past here a few days ago, on his way to the saloon down the street.'

Sumner nodded. 'Much obliged.'

He walked down to the dirty little saloon where Weeks had sat drinking not long ago with the now deceased Seger. He stood outside for a couple of minutes, listening to the muted talking of patrons inside, then pushed through the double slatted doors.

He stood just inside the entrance, looking around. Looking physical and dangerous. Very slowly patrons stopped talking and stared at Sumner warily. He walked over to the mahogany bar, his riding spurs puncturing the new silence in staccato rhythm.

'A Planter's Rye,' he told the slovenly bartender. 'And don't water it.'

'We got the best whiskey this side of Stillwater,' the barkeep replied.

'Like I said.' Sumner insisted.

The bartender brought the drink, and then swatted a fly on the bar with an ancient fly-swatter. Sumner glanced above his head and saw two strips of yellow fly-paper dotted heavily with black corpses. He swigged the drink while the bartender watched.

'I'm looking for some men,' he said then. He placed a gold coin on the bar, which greatly overpaid for the drink. 'A man named Latham. And he has two friends.'

'Never heard of him.'

'Dresses like he's going to a Grange Hall dance. Hangs around with a man with one ear.'

'Hmm. There was a man in here, I think, with one ear.'

'That was last week,' a voice came from behind Sumner. He turned to a table of card players. It was a lanky cowpoke who had spoken. 'He was drinking with another man. Name of Seger. They left together, and I hear Seger ain't been seen in here since.'

'Where did they go?' Sumner asked.

A second man at the table spoke up. 'I think One Ear

97

mentioned a house out on the main road north. The only one I can think of is the old Sutter place about a mile out of town. It's been for rent.'

'You've been a big help,' Sumner said with satisfaction.

'Friends of yours?' the first man asked.

'Something like that.' He threw more coins on to the bar. 'Drinks all around at that table,' he told the bartender.

Then he left, with the scattered patrons staring after him curiously.

Almost at that same moment at the Latham house, Latham and Sloan were preparing to leave for several hours. Latham wanted to take Sloan to Old Fort to take a look at the interior of the bank there with him. Latham was planning to hit the place within the next week. And he intended to be married by that time. The two of them were still strapping on their gunbelts when Sumner reined up a hundred yards away in a small clump of cottonwoods.

Sumner dismounted and looked the scene over carefully. Latham's and Sloan's mounts were saddled up outside at a short hitching rail, and as he had approached, he had seen Weeks' horse in a small corral behind the house. It was obvious that two of the men were leaving soon, and apparently leaving one behind, possibly to watch over Dulcie.

Sumner faced a problem choice. He could wait for the two to leave and retrieving Dulcie should be considerably easier, and more certain. But he would lose two

98

potential bounties that way, and bounties were what had brought him here. If he went on in now, confronting all three but reducing his chances of survival, he had the potential of three bounties, but placed Dulcie in a much riskier situation, one where she might never see Provost or Nebraska again.

He decided that Dulcie was more important than the bounties. And a moment later the choice was taken from him, anyway. Latham and Sloan emerged from the house. He was too far away to challenge them, and dismounted. He watched them mount up and ride off on a small road between Sumner and them. In a moment they were out of sight.

He realized he could wait, and come back when they were all there. But he had already made his choice. Also, assuming the girl was in the house somewhere, a shootout with three men might put her in danger.

'Oh hell,' he said to himself. Maybe there would be a chance at Latham later.

He mounted the stallion and rode on up to the house, openly. It was completely quiet inside. He left the horse at the hitching rail and walked up to the front door. He tried it, and it was unlocked. Very carefully he turned the knob, and pushed the door wide open.

He was facing the wide parlour, and there was nobody in sight. He stepped inside and quietly closed the door behind him. There was a doorway across the room, leading to the kitchen, and he heard a small noise come from there. A moment later Weeks came through the doorway into the parlour, chewing a bit of food and holding a cup in his right hand. He stopped dead when he saw Sumner.

'What the hell!' he exclaimed past the mouthful. He quickly swallowed it, then very slowly set the cup down on a small table near him.

'Eli Weeks, I presume,' Sumner said calmly.

'How do you know that?' His gunhand now out over his Wells Fargo.

'Where is she?' Sumner said.

'The Provost girl? Why do you care?'

'Is she in the house?'

Weeks hesitated. 'I think she's upstairs in her room. If that's any of your business. Are you a new friend of Duke?'

'Not exactly;' Sumner said. 'Actually, I came here to kill you.'

Weeks was not intimidated. 'I don't see no marshal's badge.' His eyes widened. 'By Jesus! Provost sent you!'

'The man wins a cigar.'

'And you're here to take the girl back.'

'Double hit.'

Weeks relaxed into a confrontation stance. 'Where did they find you? In some gambling hall? Well, this is your unlucky day, Dandy. I'm the fastest gun of us all. I never been beat. And if you want the girl you have to come past me. If you think you can kill me, here I am. Give it your best.' A hard grin.

'Why don't you show me how?' Sumner said in a flat voice.

In the next moment Weeks went for the Wells Fargo in a blindingly fast draw. But Sumner had read his eyes and beat him by a half-second. Both guns roared loudly in the room, making glass rattle in windows and a tin ceiling tremble above their heads. Sumner felt a hot burning on his right side, but his lead struck Weeks over the heart and punched him back against the door jamb behind him, where he hung for a moment with a look of abject surprise on his narrow face, then slid slowly to the floor.

In the next moment Dulcie came out on to the stairway at the end of the room, and stopped part-way down it. She was in her underclothes. She looked at Sumner, then stared hard at Weeks.

'Oh, my God!'

Sumner slid the big gun into its holster as if nothing had happened. He felt of his side, and found that the hit was just a shallow grazing one. His hand came away with a smear of blood on it. He looked towards Dulcie and stared for a moment at her.

'You're only sixteen?'

She self-consciously covered her cleavage. She was well clothed, though. 'Is he dead?'

'That would be my guess,' he answered, still looking her over. 'You must be Dulcie.'

She nodded absently. 'Who are you?'

'The name is Sumner. Your daddy sent me.'

Dulcie's face blossomed into a beautiful, wide smile. 'You're from Papa?' she cried out. 'I knew it, deep down! That he would find me!' She came down the stairs and threw herself at Sumner, hugging herself to him.

He grimaced with the pain in his side, but she didn't notice. She looked into his face. 'You're heaven-sent!'

she exclaimed happily. She kissed him on his cheek.

Sumner separated them gently. 'Let's hold off on that judgment till I get you back home. When do you expect the others back?'

'Not for a few hours.'

'Go get some riding clothes on. I'll saddle Weeks' mount up and you can ride that. And hurry. We don't really know how much time we have.'

Dulcie couldn't quit smiling. But there were tears of joy, too. 'You came all the way down here! I don't know how to thank you!'

'Your daddy is taking care of that,' he said. 'Now go. Get dressed.'

Dulcie walked past the lifeless Weeks, whose eyes were still staring, unseeing, across the room. 'Take that, damn you!' she muttered as she went past him.

Sumner smiled slightly.

Less than a half-hour later Dulcie was dressed in her riding pants and a frilly blouse that replaced the blue one she had torn. She also wore a narrow-brim hat found earlier in a closet trunk. By the time she appeared outside, Sumner had saddled Weeks' horse. Sumner was impressed by the way she mounted and handled her mount.

'Ready?' he asked her.

'I've been ready since they took me at Wolf Creek.'

A couple of moments later the house had disappeared from view behind them. But Dulcie never looked back.

Everything she had so desperately wished for now lay ahead of her.

SEVEN

It was three hours later when Latham and Sloan returned from Old Fort and its bank. They both now had a good idea of what to expect inside when they returned there within the week to rob it of its gold and silver. Latham was very excited about the prospect. And he expected to be married when that happened.

The two men took their mounts to the corral behind the house, and immediately saw that Weeks' horse wasn't there.

'What the hell!' Latham growled. 'If that little bastard went into town again, I'll put one in him! I mean it, Ira!'

'Maybe there was some emergency,' Sloan suggested.

They quickly unsaddled their horses, and walked to the front of the house and entered, Latham fuming. The first thing they saw was Weeks' corpse lying on the floor over by the kitchen doorway.

They both stood frozen in place for a moment. Then Sloan spoke first. 'Good Jesus!' he muttered quietly.

Latham went over to Weeks and bent over him.

'Is he dead?' Sloan asked from behind him.

103

Latham nodded. 'He's shot. Right through the heart.' He stood up and faced the stairway. A clammy fist in his chest. 'Dulcie!' he yelled out.

Complete silence answered him. In the next moment he was running up the stairs, while Sloan waited below still staring at Weeks. Then Latham was coming back down, his aquiline face looking haggard. He came and sat down heavily on a chair. 'She's gone!' Talking to himself.

Sloan sat down on the sofa facing him. 'Somebody came for her. And Weeks got in the way.' He glanced over at the dead body with its staring eyes.

'Who the hell even knew we were here?' Latham wondered.

'Provost sent somebody to find us,' Sloan guessed. 'And he did.'

'That doesn't seem possible,' Latham said dully. 'We didn't leave a trace. Maybe it's somebody from town. Hears about the girl out here and decided to steal her from us.'

'I think it's Provost.' Sloan said.

Latham looked over at him. 'I hate to admit it, but you must be right. But who would he hire that could find us down here? A rogue Territory marshal?'

'A bounty hunter,' Sloan surmised. 'Some of them are pretty good at tracking people down.'

'We don't have worthwhile bounties on us.'

'Provost could put that right,' Sloan insisted.

'Damn, you're right. Of course you are,' Latham said, sitting forward tensely and kneading his fists. 'Some sonofabitch rode all the way from Nebraska, killed Weeks, and grabbed Dulcie.'

'Let him have her, Duke. You made your point with Provost. You're better off without her.'

Latham looked over at him. 'I'm going after her, Ira.'

Sloan frowned heavily, turned away from him and swore. 'Goddam it, Duke. You have to get this female out of your system. This obsession could wreck the rest of your life if you let it.'

'You can call it what you want.' Latham said deliberately. 'But she isn't Provost's any more, Ira. She's mine, and always will be. I still intend to put a gold ring on her finger. Here, or somewhere else. I'd track her to the South Pole if I had to.'

Sloan was shaking his head. 'They have a half-day's ride on you. You'd have to ride hard to catch them.'

'I intend to start now. I'll find them in two or three days, I promise you. I'll ride day and night if I have to. And I want you with me.'

Sloan shook his head again. 'I don't want no part of it. I didn't like it from the very beginning. You should have gone after Provost, not his daughter.'

'Don't you see how much better this is than just killing that pea-brain rancher? You kill him and it's over in a minute. This way he has his whole life to suffer. No, this is much better.'

'Well, I'm not going,' Sloan said harshly.

Latham narrowed his eyes on him. 'Have I ever double-crossed you, Ira? In any way?'

'Can't say you have.'

'Haven't I made you a lot of money since we started riding together?'

Sloan sighed. 'We've done pretty well.'

'I've got big plans, Ira. The Old Fort thing is out now. But the banks are even richer other places. I promise you, stick with me and I'll make you rich.'

'Three makes a crowd, Duke, if you get her back.'

Latham rose from his chair, and stood over Sloan. 'Let me talk plain to you, Ira. I'd take it as a personal insult if you left me at this crucial time. An act of disloyalty.' In a menacing tone.

Sloan stared up at him. 'Are you threatening me, Duke? Me, Ira?'

'Make it as you wish. But I need you now. Like you've needed me so many times before. Tell you what. Ride with me till I find her and you can do what you want then. I won't oppose you.'

Sloan sat there. 'I could shoot you in your sleep, you know.'

'You're not the type,' Latham said, with a small grin.

Sloan blew his cheeks out. 'All right. Maybe I do owe you. But when you find her, it's over, Duke.'

Latham nodded. 'I'm sorry to hear that. But it's OK. Now, let's get those animals saddled up. You get some grub together, for the trail. Then we're out of here. There's a lot of riding time left today.'

Sloan rose heavily. 'Right, I'll be ready within the half-hour.'

Several hours later the sky was getting dark. Sumner and Dulcie had ridden hard to put some distance between them and Latham. They came to a junction of trails, and Sumner reined up. Dulcie came up beside him.

'Are we making camp?' she wondered.

He was looking off to the west, along the other trail. 'No. How are you doing?'

'You ride hard. I'm pretty tired.'

'You're doing fine. Let's get off the trail and give the horses a short rest.'

He led her over to a clump of saplings and they dismounted there. They went and leaned against a couple of mesquites together.

'Will he come after you?' Sumner asked her.

She nodded. She had her auburn hair in a braid behind her head, and looked very young to him. Her cheeks were flushed from the precipitous departure. 'I think so.'

'So do I. That's why we rode so hard.'

She arched her back and stretched: 'You got there just in time. He planned to marry me in the next few days. I'd have been in his bed every night.' She sneaked a look at him to see his reaction.

He was impassive. 'You have some colour under your eye. Did he do that?'

'He beat me regularly. He's kind of crazy about things being just right. If I didn't do things just the way he wanted, I'd often get physically beaten. Sometimes he even used his fist. Or a strap.'

Sumner looked sombre. He had made the right decision back there, to put Dulcie's welfare first. 'Did he . . . molest you?'

She shook her head. 'For some reason, I think he was saving me for his marriage to me.'

'What about the others?'

'Duke kept them off me. Weeks brought another

man in one day, though, and things started happening. But Duke came back with Sloan. That other man ended up buried behind the house.'

Sumner was shaking his head. 'Sorry about all that. But it could have been much worse, as I'm sure you know. I'm glad I came.'

She gave him a big smile. 'So am I.'

'Now it's up to me to see that you get back to Provost safe. Till we ride on to that ranch together, I want you to stick to me like glue. I don't want you out of my sight. Understand?'

Dulcie looked him over good for the first time. She liked the looks of him. She gave him a very lovely smile. 'That sounds very nice.'

He didn't respond. Over thirty, he considered her a child. And he pushed it out of his head that she looked like a woman. A very desirable one.

'Latham will think we're heading straight north, on this route that brought us all here. So I'm turning west now to throw him off. There's a little town west of here most of a day's ride called Post Supply. A cow trail goes through there also going north, but quite a distance from here. We'll take that route north.'

The smile faded on Dulcie's pretty face. 'Well, wait a minute. We'd be losing a day to put that many more miles between us and him. I want to get as far north as I can as fast as I can.'

Sumner was beginning to learn what Latham already knew. She was a girl who knew her own mind. She had been raised that way by Provost.

He sighed. 'Dulcie. You're not back on that ranch yet.

You're in my charge now. You do what I tell you till we get back. And we might just get there.'

She stuck her chin out. 'Well, I have a say in this. I'm your boss's daughter, you know. And I feel safer continuing north. Otherwise, we're giving the ground back that we've just ridden so hard to gain.'

He gave her a narrow look. 'First of all, your daddy isn't my boss. And second, this isn't a democracy where you get a vote. From now on till we get back to Nebraska, I call the shots. If you give me trouble, I'll tie you up till we get there.'

Dulcie frowned heavily. 'Now you sound like Duke Latham.'

He sighed. 'Get mounted,' he told her. 'We're riding on. West.'

Dulcie hesitated, then mounted her horse. 'You're a bully,' she commented. 'Are you an ex-lawman?'

He got on the stallion. He looked over at her, figuring she might as well know. 'I hunt down men like Latham for the rewards on them.'

Her face changed. 'Oh. Do you turn them in to the authorities?'

'No, I don't.'

'Ever?'

'Ever.'

She looked him over again as if for the first time. 'Oh, God!'

'Let's go, Dulcie. We still have a lot of ground to cover tonight.'

Almost three hours later, Latham and Sloan were galloping towards that intersection at full speed, taking

almost no notice of crossroads. But Sumner and Dulcie
were already halfway to Post Supply.

It was just past two in the morning when Sumner reined
in about a half-mile short of Post Supply. They could see
the outskirts of the small town ahead of them on the trail.

Dulcie was slumping in her saddle, worn out. 'Why
are we stopping? There's the town up ahead.'

'We're not going in. Not tonight,' he said.

'Why not?'

'If we didn't fool Latham, he'll ask about us there.
We'll make hardship camp over by that little creek
there.'

'Make camp? I'm ready to fall off my horse. I need a
bed to sleep in tonight! I deserve it, damn it, after what
you've put me through!'

Sumner regarded her soberly, and his voice softened.
'Of course you do. Don't you think I know that? You've
been great, Dulcie. You've got grit, and I like that. But
every move we make now is a life or death decision.'

Dulcie sighed. 'Oh, God.'

But she followed him over to the stream where there
was a stand of young poplars, and they made camp.
Sumner did most of the work, but she put a coffee pot
on the fire, and Sumner had some hardtack in his
saddle-bag – and that was it. They sat on their saddles by
the fire, but when Sumner reached for the pot, she saw
him grimace slightly, and then she saw the blood on his
shirt where Weeks had shot him.

'Oh, my God! You're hurt!'

He looked down at his shirt. 'Oh. It's nothing. It's

scabbing over already.'

'Weeks?'

He nodded. 'Fortunately he's not much of a shot.'

Once again, Dulcie was staring hard at him. For the first time she began to understand the danger he had placed himself in, to rescue her. 'I'm . . . sorry. I guess I kind of took you for granted. That was dumb of me.'

He sipped at his coffee. 'I'm being well paid, Dulcie.'

'Even so,' she said. She sipped her coffee quietly. 'I owe you my life.'

'Why don't we hold off judgment on that?' he smiled at her.

'I don't even know your first name.'

'It's Wesley. I rarely hear it called.'

She looked at him over her coffee cup. 'You're very good-looking, you know.'

He laughed lightly. 'That's about the last way anybody else would describe me.'

'How do most people see you?'

'Well, the first thing they see is this Peacemaker I wear. And then they try to remember the things they've heard about the way I use it.'

A little thrill of awe rippled through her. 'Are you that good with it?'

'Nobody's beaten me yet. Now let's change the subject.'

'I think I see why Papa hired you.'

'We just ran on to each other. When he was out looking for you.'

She looked into the fire. 'I acted like a kid back there.'

'You are a kid.'

'I'll be more co-operative. I promise.'

'That will help,' he told her.

'Do you really see me as a kid?' With a seductive smile.

He studied her for a moment. 'As Latham noticed, you're physically grown up, Dulcie. But that doesn't make you a woman. Not yet.'

She was disappointed. 'Don't you think I'm pretty?'

He shook his head. 'Dulcie. Forget your looks and start giving serious thought to survival. Your life may depend on it.'

'Sorry.'

He put their bedrolls out a little later and they got a few much needed hours of sleep before the sun rose in colourful hues in the morning.

They rode right through Post Supply that morning. It was a dry, dusty little town just south of the border with Kansas. There was a saloon and a hotel, but Sumner had no intention of stopping at either of them. He did stop at a small general store, letting Dulcie wait outside, and bought some provisions for the trail – matches, lard, beef jerky, coffee, and a few tinned goods. He bought Dulcie a vest to wear over her blouse, for warmth. He also had a jacket he could lend her.

Nobody paid any attention to them in town, and they were out on the trail again within the hour, but this time turning north. There was no unnecessary banter between them when they were riding: Sumner cut her off any time she began a conversation. It was particularly important to make good ground now since they had taken the detour west.

When Latham and Sloan had reached the crossroad where Sumner and Dulcie had turned off, they went galloping past it without giving it any notice. Latham was certain that Dulcie and her captor must be just ahead somewhere, and that he would be catching them at any moment. In another hour though, he began to have doubts. They had passed a couple of towns on their wild ride, but avoided them just as he figured his pursued quarry would.

Now, at about the time that Sumner and Dulcie were riding out of Post Supply, Latham dusted to a stop near the same small stream he had camped beside on his way south. He and Sloan had ridden all night, and Sloan was fatigued and irritated.

Latham slid off his mount, tore his hat off, and threw it on to the ground. Sloan watched him sullenly from his horse.

'That little bitch! Where is she?'

'I need some sleep,' Sloan said bitterly. 'You drove us all night, and what did it get us? They didn't come this way.'

'What?' Latham barked out.

'We'd have caught them by now. They're not on this trail. Unless they're bold enough to stop in one of them towns we passed up.'

'Whoever this is, if he was smart enough to find us, he wouldn't do that.'

'They could have gone south,' Sloan said, dismounting. 'He could have arranged with Provost to wire him from Mexico. Or Austin. So Provost could come with a small army to get her.'

'Their tracks headed out north.'

'That could have been a ruse. I'm just saying. They could be anywhere. They're sure as hell not in front of us. I said I'd stick it out till you found her, Duke. But this is ridiculous. We have no clue. Look, things are different now. Let's give it up and ride up to Dodge. I know a couple of people there that could get us a fresh start there in Kansas.'

Latham fairly yelled at him. 'I'm not interested in making a new start, goddam it! Not till this is over!'

Sloan slumped into himself, and leaned against his mount's flanks, which were foamy with sweat. 'You don't need her, Duke.'

Latham looked out over the trail. 'I know that now.'

Sloan squinted down at him. 'What?'

'I no longer want to marry that little baby Provost. When we catch her, I'm going to put one in her. Then I'll wire Provost and tell him where he can come and get her.'

Sloan was studying him sombrely. 'You mean that?'

'I'll still have my payback to Provost. Maybe this will even be better. He'll have to bury his only kid.'

'And I was beginning to think you had a thing for her.'

'You were right. Taking her to bed got all mixed up with getting back at Provost. I went a little crazy. But that wasn't the real Duke Latham. What you see before you now, is. Now – I think he took a different route north.'

Sloan nodded. He was energized, thinking this might

114

be over soon, and without having to put up with the girl as a live-in. 'Come to think of it, if I was him I might have gone a more westerly route. There are more towns on the way, and they wouldn't be afraid to use them because we wouldn't be behind them.'

'We'll try to get a little sleep. Then we're riding west,' Latham announced. 'I've also got a strong hunch that's where we'll find them. Then it will be the end of the trail for that little Provost puppy.'

'That suits me right down to my boots,' Sloan muttered.

It was a long day later when Sumner and Dulcie rode into Cimarron, Kansas. They had left the Territory about midday, and Dulcie hoped she never saw it again.

Cimarron was a sizeable town west of Dodge City, on a cow trail. There were a couple of decent hotels, several saloons, and a number of stores and shops. Women were walking the main street under parasols, and carriages and buggies moved up and down the dusty thoroughfare. It was late afternoon and too early for cowboy festivities in the saloons, so the town appeared quite tranquil.

They needed more provisions for the trail, and Sumner decided to purchase ammunition for the Colt he carried, so he reined up before a small general store.

'I'll have to buy some things in here,' he told Dulcie. 'Then we'll be riding on through.'

Dulcie was heavily fatigued. She took her hat off and wiped at her forehead. Even under these circumstances she looked very pretty. She turned to Sumner with a frown. 'Duke might be over in Wichita by now,' she complained. 'Why can't we stop overnight at that nice hotel across the street?'

Sumner dismounted, looking very dangerous in his dark clothes and the Peacemaker on his hip. Two women were approaching on the board sidewalk, and when they got a look at him, they crossed the street. He was feeling out of sorts, nurse-maiding Dulcie and trying to make good time on the trail, and he looked tough and belligerent. He looked up at Dulcie in irritation.

'I told you, Dulcie. It's dangerous to be seen at a hotel or saloon. That's where Latham would ask. And we have no idea where he is. He could be right behind us by an hour or two. That's why I don't camp near the trail. We only have to make one mistake, and it could be over for you. It's your life that's on the line. Don't forget that.'

She sighed heavily. 'Maybe you're being unnecessarily careful.'

'Well, that's something that's on me. You have no say-so in it.' Before she could respond he hitched the stallion and went into the store.

Dulcie swore mildly under her breath and dismounted. A moment later she was up on the narrow porch of the store and leaning against the façade there. She was hot, her face flushed a little. She removed her hat again and her auburn hair shone in the late sun. Around her face it was damp.

Two drifters emerged from a saloon a short distance away, and were talking and laughing as they approached her. They looked like rough types, with worn clothing and guns on their hips. The tall, lanky one of the two spotted Dulcie when they came nearer, and nudged his heavier partner.

'Hey. Look at that! I didn't see nothing like that in the saloon.'

A big grin from the hefty man. 'I wonder if she's friendly.'

They walked on up to Dulcie, and she noticed them for the first time. She looked them over with disdain.

'Hi, honey,' the tall fellow grinned at her. 'What are you doing out here all by your lonesome?'

Despite her fatigue, a little tension built in her. 'I'm waiting for a friend,' she said quietly. Looking at them, visions of Latham and his men flitted darkly through her head. 'Now please move on.'

The hefty one grunted out a laugh. 'Waiting for a friend? I don't give that credence, sweetheart. I think you was waiting for us.'

They were in her face now, very close, and she was becoming very uncomfortable. 'I asked you to leave,' she said tightly. 'If you won't, I will.' She started past the tall man towards the door of the store. But he stepped into her path.

'Now just a minute, darling. We want to talk a minute, and you're being downright rude to us. Say, you're a young one, ain't you? We like them young, don't we, Gus?'

'The younger the juicier,' Gus grinned. She could smell alcohol on his breath.

'Let me past!' she exclaimed then, trying to push past the tall man.

But he caught her arm and held it in a vice-like grip,

hurting her. 'Why don't we take a little walk together, honey? Out in back of this building here. We just want to talk.'

'Let go of me!' she cried out. 'Wesley!'

'Who?' the tall man frowned.

'She's just making him up,' Gus ventured, grinning.

But in a moment Sumner emerged from the store, stared hard at them, and turned to face them. A few paces away. Looking grim and deadly.

'Evening, boys. Anything we can do for you?'

The tall man released his hold on Dulcie, and faced Sumner. He and Gus had had just enough dark ale to be injudicious in their behaviour. 'Oh. The friend. Yeah, you can just go back in there and get your buying done, and turn her over to us for a little while.'

Sumner sighed and came a few steps closer. 'You boys got bounties on your ugly heads?'

Now both men were facing him. Taking notice of the big Peacemaker, and the svelte look of him.

'Why is that any of your business?' Gus growled at him.

But the tall one was studying Sumner more carefully. 'Wait. Did she call you Wesley a minute ago?'

Dulcie was rubbing her arm, and feeling a lot better. 'That's right,' she offered smugly.

The tall man was putting two and two together. 'Wesley. Bounties.' His face sagged into a look of dismay. 'My God. You're Certainty Sumner!'

Gus looked over at his partner. 'Huh?'

Now Sumner was doubly irritated. He did not want to be recognized on this flight north. 'Move away from

118

her,' he said quietly.

The tall man took two steps backward so fast he almost fell. Gus, now understanding too, joined him. A small smile came on to Dulcie's pretty face, and her awe of Sumner grew. Sumner turned to her. 'Are you all right?'

'I'm fine. Now that you're here.'

Sumner turned to the two assailants. 'Just a suggestion. You probably ought to get the hell out of here. While you still can.'

The tall man nodded quickly. 'We're already gone.' A tight grin.

'Good meeting you,' Gus offered.

'Move,' Sumner growled.

Gus nodded this time, and they hurried away, towards a second saloon.

Sumner turned to Dulcie again. 'You better come inside with me. You'll attract men like flies to a honey-pot.'

She liked that. She gave him a sexy smile. 'I'm glad you think so.'

He ignored the flirting. 'There's a camp stool in there I might buy for you.'

She put her hat back on. 'I didn't know. That you could do that.'

'Oh, them? They're everywhere. But they're seldom any real trouble.'

'I see that.' She smiled at him.

He gave her a sober look. 'Come on, Dulcie. We've already stayed here too long.'

That evening they made hardship camp a few miles

119

north of Cimarron, and off the trail. Dulcie helped make a fire, and then cooked them a light meal while Sumner tended to the horses. After they were finished and the implements were cleaned up and put away, they sat at the fire side by side, Dulcie on her new folding stool. They sipped at coffee cups and stared into the fire.

'I'm very impressed,' Dulcie finally said.

Sumner looked over at her. They were hatless, and a lock of dark hair had fallen on to his face. He didn't respond.

'I mean, here we are down in Kansas and those men knew about you. And they were scared to death of you.'

'They used good judgment,' he said.

She was studying his aquiline face from the light of the fire. 'I've never met anyone like you,' she said softly.

He met her look. 'You're a bit different yourself, Dulcie.'

'Do you think so?'

'I usually say what I mean.'

'You've never married?'

He frowned. 'Does it matter?'

'I just want to know more about you.' She paused. 'I like you.'

His frown disappeared. He took a deep breath in. 'There was a girl once. But when I went to her to ask her to marry me, after a long absence, she was already married.' A wry smile.

'I'm sorry.'

'I had no other plans about my future. I grabbed the first wanted dodger I saw, stuffed it in my pocket, and never looked back.' He stared out into the blackness. 'I had already killed five men, for various reasons that I felt were valid. And I had learned some skill with a gun.'

Her face had changed. 'I see.'

Sumner caught her eye. 'I'm not a murderer, Dulcie. I only hunt killers, and they always have a fair chance to defend themselves.'

'I don't see anything wrong in it. I guess Papa didn't, either.'

'It's a kind of life,' he said.

She stretched her legs out in front of the fire. 'For a woman out here, there's only one life available to her. She's expected to marry and have children and make a home for her husband.'

'And you'd like more than that?'

'I think I'd like to work on a newspaper for a while. Maybe have a column of my own.'

He poked at the fire with a stick, and sparks flew up into the dark. 'You must be a reader.'

She smiled gratefully at his understanding. 'I am. I like Jane Austen, and Herman Melville.'

He glanced over at her. '*Moby Dick*?'

Her lovely smile brightened. 'Why, yes. Do you know it?'

'I read it in prison.'

The smile faded. 'You were in prison?'

'Three of the men I told you about earlier. They raped and murdered my aunt, and I went after them. It was all justified. But the law sent me up anyway.'

A heavy silence fell into the camp area for a long moment.

121

'I think I'm really beginning to like you, Wesley,' she finally said soberly.

A frown edged its way on to his face. 'Dulcie. What are you saying?'

'You know what I'm saying.'

He shook his head slowly. 'Dulcie, what's in your head? It's natural to feel gratitude for being rescued from that low-life. But don't mix that up with anything else. You're just a kid. When you get back, you'll be dating boys your own age. And that's proper. Don't confuse gratitude with affection.'

'I can't help it. I do have affection for you. Don't you feel just a little something for me?'

He sighed. 'Of course I do.' He avoided looking at her lovely face, and the way she filled out her clothes. 'But not in that way. I'm not a goddam child molester. Like Latham. Maybe we better change the subject.'

'I may be young. But I think you know I look like a woman. And I have the feelings of a woman.'

'Keep on with this and I'll have to gag you.' He stood up and walked over to the horses.

'I'm not virginal, you know.'

'Goddam it, Dulcie!' he said heatedly, turning back to her.

'There was this neighbour boy. About a year ago. He took me out behind the barn. Papa doesn't know.' She smiled to herself.

He walked over to the fire, facing her sombrely. 'Did you forget who's in charge here?'

'Of course not.'

'Then get this straight. Between you and me it's

strictly business, and always will be. Get any other ideas out of your little head. Once and for all.'

She looked away from him, her eyes watering up. 'If that's the way you want it.'

He was about to change the subject when he heard a voice behind him, from a small stand of trees.

'I thought I'd find you out here.'

Sumner turned quickly, and Dulcie rose from her stool. Sumner had started for his gun, but found a long revolver aimed at his chest. It was a rough-looking man on horseback, and he had quietly come up on them as Sumner's attention was diverted by Dulcie. Sumner swore under his breath.

'Oh!' Dulcie gasped.

'Who the hell are you?' Sumner growled out.

'I'm Gus's brother. The boy you hoorawed earlier in town. My family won't tolerate that from no gunslinger. So here I am.'

'Oh, God,' Dulcie whispered.

'You've got it all wrong, mister,' Sumner told him. 'Your brother was harassing this girl here. I asked him to leave.'

'You made him back down,' the stranger said in a deep, hostile voice. He was a big man, with several days' growth of beard and a scar through his right eyebrow. 'Now that has to be answered.'

Dulcie was getting her courage back. 'Do you know who this is?'

'I know, girlie. And that makes it all the sweeter.'

Sumner sighed. 'You don't have to do this.'

'Yes, I do. Now, step away from the girl. I want to keep

her healthy.'

Dulcie swallowed new fear back.

Sumner stepped slowly away from Dulcie, as he spoke again. 'All right. But she has a gun, too.' As he stepped into the line of fire.

As Sumner expected, the gunman's eyes went to Dulcie for just a second. And in that second, Sumner drew the Peacemaker.

His attacker saw the lightning-fast movement at the last moment, but his reaction time was too slow. The big Colt roared in the darkness three times in rapid succession, punching Gus's brother in the belly, over the heart, and in the left eye.

The attacker's and Dulcie's bodies jumped with each shot, and he was knocked backwards off his horse, which reared and ran off into the night. Sumner stood there relaxed and motionless. Then he twirled the Colt over twice until it rested snugly in its holster.

Dulcie stood with her jaw dropped slightly open. She had not seen him kill Weeks, so she had never seen him in action. 'My God. You're as good as they all think you are.'

'I'm sorry you had to see that. But he gave me no choice.' He went over and examined the very dead body on the ground. 'He should have let it go.' He went over to the fire and poured himself a cup of hot coffee. 'Can I get you one?'

Dulcie was almost speechless. 'I think I'll wait till I can move my arms and legs again,' she said with a weak smile.

EIGHT

It was an overcast, damp morning in Cimarron when Duke Latham and Ira Sloan rode into that cowtown. It was just past seven, and Sumner and Dulcie had broken camp and headed on north less than an hour before, just a mile beyond town.

Latham and Sloan had ridden most of the night to get there, but had no idea they were now so close to their quarry.

The saloons were still closed up, so Latham could not inquire at any of them. They reined up, therefore, in front of a hotel down the street from one of the saloons. There were very few pedestrians out on the street. Latham leaned on his saddlehorn and removed his Stetson.

'I'm ready to quit this,' Sloan grumbled. 'This is getting us nothing, Duke.'

'You'll quit when I quit,' Latham growled at him. 'Stay put here. I'll inquire in here. I got a feeling. That we're getting close.'

'All right. But when you're through with that, let's

125

stop at that little restaurant we saw down the street. I could eat the nails in my boots.'

'I'll just take a minute,' Latham told him.

He wrapped his reins over a hitching post and went into the hotel. As the miles wore on, his anger towards Dulcie had grown. Now, in his head, he was raping her before killing her, and maybe even letting Sloan have a turn on her. Then he would leave her body in a woods somewhere where Provost could find it, when Latham broke the news to him by telegram.

Inside the hotel, it was Kansas City luxury. Potted palms. Carpeting. A Remington painting on the wall behind the desk. There was a fat clerk behind a mahogany counter.

'May I help you, sir?' Tilting his head down to look at them over his reading glasses.

'I'm looking for a couple of friends. A man and young woman travelling together. Has anybody like that been in here the past couple of nights?'

'I believe there was a couple here two nights ago,' the clerk said curtly. 'If they're your friends, you missed them. Can I get you a room?'

Latham took quick interest. 'A couple? How did they register? What names?'

'Oh, I can't tell you that, sir. It's against hotel policy. Do you intend to stay the night?'

Latham walked around the end of the counter and went over to the clerk.

'Oh! You can't be back here, sir! We don't allow that!'

Latham grabbed him by the shirt and pushed him back against a bank of key boxes. The fellow winced

126

when he hit them, his breath coming hard. 'Please!'

'What were their names?' Latham spat at him.

The clerk swallowed back his fear. 'Why, I believe it was Watkins.'

'What did they look like?'

'Well, let's see. They was well dressed. I remember she was very courteous.'

Latham fairly shouted at him. 'Damn it, how old were they?'

'Oh, they both had grey hair. I think he was a banker from Wichita.'

Latham swore under his breath. 'Why the hell didn't you say so?'

He released his hold on the clerk and stormed out of the lobby, grumbling under his breath. Outside, he went down and leaned on his mount's flank. Sloan watched him silently.

'They haven't been there.'

Sloan shook his head. 'Let's go eat,' he said dully.

They walked down to the small restaurant, found a table at the front of the place, and ordered breakfast. Sloan was so hungry he ordered steak and eggs. But Latham had lost his appetite.

When their food was delivered, they ate in silence, Sloan wolfing his food down and Latham doing a lot of staring across the room, thinking. Wondering if they really were on the right track to catch Dulcie and her captor.

'We could head back east and see if they went through Dodge,' Sloan finally offered, as he finished up his plate. Latham was sipping at a cup of coffee.

'They came this way. I feel it in my bones,' he said quietly.

There was only one other table occupied, by a local man and wife, and they now paid their bill and left.

Finally Sloan looked over at Latham. 'We're not going to find them.' he said flatly. 'I feel that in my bones.'

Latham regarded him darkly. 'If she makes it back to Provost, I swear to God I'll ride in there and shoot him down like a goddam dog!'

'You'd never get past his men,' Sloan said.

Latham thought about that. 'Then I'd go out and kill somebody. Anybody. Just to get it out of my system.'

Sloan gave him a narrow look, but said nothing. In the next moment, the door opened and two men came in. One was Gus, the fellow who had harassed Dulcie in town the previous day, and whose brother now lay dead out on the trail where Sumner had killed him. Gus was with a blocky man who worked for a local blacksmith. They took a table not far from Latham and Sloan. The proprietor came and took their order and left. Latham was still nursing the coffee, and thinking dark thoughts.

'He left last night,' Gus was saying. 'But Natty says he ain't been back since.'

'Well, don't that beat all,' the other man retorted. 'What do you think, Gus?'

'I don't know, but I better ride out there later. Take a couple of dependable boys with me.'

Neither Latham nor Sloan was paying any attention to them. Sloan let out a long breath. 'I wish I could get you off this, Duke. It could wreck our future plans. We got big money to make. You had some good ideas.'

'That will all come, don't worry,' Latham said absently. 'Once I get my payback. Everything will be good again.'

Across the way, Gus was speaking again. 'We had no idea who he was. Till the girl called his name.'

'And you say it was somebody named Sumner?'

'That's right. Just maybe the most dangerous gunslinger out there. Well, we wasn't going up against that. But that just got in Ben's craw. So he went out to take him by surprise.'

Latham turned to Sloan. 'Did you hear that? That bounty hunter and a girl. Sonofabitch.'

'Certainty Sumner?' Sloan wondered.

But Latham had already risen from his chair and was on his way over to the other table. When he got there he leaned over Gus. 'I heard you talking over here. Did you meet up with a man named Certainty Sumner?'

Gus gave him a dismissive look. 'Who the hell are you?'

'Somebody you don't want to get crossways of. Now, just answer the question.'

Gus frowned. 'Are you with the city marshal?'

Latham sighed, and drew his Starr .44 and shoved the muzzle up against Gus's right temple.

'Hey!' Gus exclaimed.

'Take it easy, stranger,' the blacksmith said, a little breathlessly.

'Now, when I ask you a question, I want an answer, understand?'

Gus swallowed hard. 'I got it.'

'Then answer my question.'

'It was that bounty hunter, all right. Sure enough.'

'And he was with somebody?'

'A girl. Just a kid, but a looker.'

Latham grunted. 'You tell me true, you little weasel, or I'll blow that tiny brain of yours out past your left ear. Did he call her name?'

Gus's tongue was paper dry. 'I . . . don't think so.'

'Did they ride out to the north?'

Gus nodded tightly. 'I believe so. My brother went after them. He ain't back yet.'

Latham finally holstered the Starr. 'Your brother is dead,' he said. Then he returned to his table.

'Did you get all of that?' he asked Sloan.

Sloan nodded. 'That's her, for sure. And Provost sent that bounty hunter after her.'

Latham grinned for the first time in days. 'Now what do you think of my gut feelings, Ira? We're right behind them, by God!' He slammed his right fist into his other hand. 'We'll catch them within forty-eight hours.'

Sloan rose from his chair. 'Then let's get on it,' he responded. 'I want this over with.'

Then they left the restaurant, with Gus and his companion staring hard after them.

Several hours later Sumner and Dulcie stopped under the shade of some young cottonwoods and dismounted. Sumner had seen she was tired and decided to give her a brief noon break. They made a small fire and heated up some coffee, and leaned against two saplings while they refreshed themselves.

'Sorry I have to push you so hard,' Sumner said to her.

'I know you're just trying to take care of me.'

They talked about their past for a few minutes, and then, without warning, Dulcie quietly said, 'I think I'm falling in love with you.'

A deep frown. 'Damn it, Dulcie! What the hell!'

She hung her head and her eyes filled with tears. 'I'm sorry.'

He walked over to her and held her arms. 'Jesus. Don't cry.'

On impulse she reached up and kissed him softly on his mouth. He was taken by surprise, but quickly moved her away from him. He had been unthinkingly receptive.

'Oh, God,' he muttered, shaking his head.

'I had to do that. I might not get another chance.'

Sumner turned away from her, getting himself under control.

'You liked it, didn't you?' she said in a half-whisper.

He turned back to her. 'Dulcie. That will never happen again.'

She smiled a lovely smile. 'Are you quite sure?'

'Nothing like that will happen between us. Now, or ever.'

She sighed heavily. 'Why didn't Papa send somebody else?' To herself.

'Never mind,' he said sombrely. 'Come on, saddle up. We're losing time.'

Less than two hours behind them, Duke Latham and Sloan stopped under the shade of a tall willow tree beside a small stream, and let their mounts take water. They both retrieved their canteens to quench their own growing thirst. Latham turned to Sloan, making his saddle leather squeak under his weight. His face was sweaty from hard riding.

'I'd bet my horse and saddle they're just ahead of us. They're probably trying to get to Atwood. That's where we'll catch them, in town or on the trail on either side. I can't wait.'

Sloan stuffed his canteen back into a saddlebag. 'Don't forget who you're confronting. This is Certainty Sumner. They say he's good.'

'Bounty hunters' reputations are always blown way up,' Latham said. Sloan noticed that as they came closer to their quarry, Latham was changing. His face seemed flushed a lot of the time, and he had a new, wild glistening in his eyes that was slightly disturbing to Sloan. Latham continued: 'And I haven't ever been beat in a draw-down, Ira. And we have two guns against his. Don't worry, he'll go down. Then that little bitch will be mine again.'

'Well, I hope it's worth it,' Sloan offered.

'Oh, it will be. You can take that to the bank,' Latham grinned brightly. 'Now. Let's get riding. We might even catch them before Atwood.'

'We'll see, Duke,' Sloan commented, studying Latham's emotional face. 'We'll see.'

A couple of hours later, Sumner and Dulcie were riding along the border of a green woods, making good time, when suddenly Sumner reined in. 'Hold it!' he said to

132

Dulcie, riding just behind him.

She came up beside him. 'What is it?'

'We're going to have company.' He pointed to a small group of riders in the distance.

Dulcie focused on them as they drew nearer. 'Can we avoid them?'

'No. It's too late.' He glanced over at her. 'Button your vest up. And pull your hat down low.'

'Why?'

'Just do it, Dulcie.'

She followed his instructions as the riders came into closer view. There were three men, and they were rough-looking characters wearing guns. Sumner reined in and Dulcie followed suit.

'They look like *mestisos*,' Sumner said quietly. 'Half-breeds. There's a bunch of them in the Territory and Kansas. They do illegal trading with Indian tribes and traffickers. You keep quiet and let me talk.'

Dulcie nodded. 'All right.' In a tense undertone.

A couple of moments later the three men halted just twenty feet away from them, kicking up dust. Barring the couple's path on the trail.

They were dark-skinned, bearded men, all husky-looking with hard eyes. The one in the middle had a scar across his jaw, his hair was braided behind his head, and he wore a bowler hat.

'Greetings, strangers! Do you speak Spanish?' In an accent.

'Not really,' Sumner answered for them. 'Nice to meet you boys. But we have business in Atwood and must be on our way.'

'Whoa! Not so fast, *amigo*!' the same man exclaimed. He seemed to be their leader. 'You have a minute for a friendly palaver, I'm sure.'

Sumner judged him to be Mexican, but the other two looked like part Pawnee or Apache. 'We don't have time for palaver,' he said easily.

Already Dulcie was getting tense. She didn't like the scrutiny she was receiving from all three of them.

'You don't understand,' the first one continued. 'We are traders, you see. You know. *Vendadores*. We buy just about anything. To sell at the big markets, you know.' He looked over at Dulcie, and the grin slid slightly off his face. His companions kept their silence.

'We have nothing to sell,' Sumner told him.

'Oh, sure! Everybody has something to sell! For the right price, you know. We ourselves have goods in our bags you might be interested in, in trade for something of yours.'

'I told you. We have no interest. We must get on to Atwood.' He started around them, spurring the stallion lightly, but one of the cohorts moved his mount into his path.

Sumner sighed. 'Look. We don't want any trouble. But we really have nothing to trade or sell. Now, if you don't mind.'

'Slow down, amigo!' the Mexican laughed. 'We don't want to give you no trouble. We want to be friendly. Don't you need blankets? I can sell a nice gold ring to the lady for half what it would cost at Fort Griffin.'

'We're moving on,' Sumner said impatiently.

'No, no. Listen. I'll buy the lady's horse for two

134

hundred dollars. Three hundred for the stallion. You can hitch a ride with the next wagon.'

'Get out of our way,' Sumner growled at him.

'All right, all right. How about this deal?' The grin had left his face. 'We'll give you one thousand dollars for the girl, her horse and her saddle.'

'You fools!' Dulcie blurted out. 'This is Certainty Sumner!'

'Be quiet,' Sumner told her quietly. 'Now, we're riding on. Don't try to stop us.'

One of the half-breeds came up to the Mexican and whispered in his ear. The Mexican's face changed, going very sober. 'So. You are a notorious bounty hunter. We hate bounty hunters.'

'I'll bet you do,' Sumner retorted. 'But we're still leaving.'

'We could shoot you down and take everything. Including the girl.'

'Not before I take at least two of you with me,' Sumner said in a low, hard voice. 'And you'll be the first one to take lead.'

Dulcie held her breath as the Mexican absorbed that threat. Finally, after what seemed like an hour to her, the Mexican spoke again.

'Hey. We was just palavering, *sí*? If we can't make a deal, you can be on your way. For your business in Atwood. And *vaya con Dios*!'

'Thanks for the well-wishes,' Sumner said acidly.

A moment later they were on their way again, and in a few minutes the knot of men was out of sight behind them.

'I stalled as long as I could,' Sumner told Dulcie as they rode side by side. 'I didn't want lead to fly, with you there.'

'Are you glad I spoke up?' she smiled at him.

He sighed. 'Yes, Dulcie. You helped. Thanks.'

'It makes me so proud. To be riding with you.'

He ignored her as if she hadn't spoken. 'We ought to be in Atwood by late night. Can you ride that long?'

'I'd follow you anywhere,' she said, not looking at him. Then they rode on in silence.

NINE

It was getting close to midnight when Sumner and Dulcie arrived in Atwood.

It had been a long, hard day, and Sumner had pushed Dulcie more than he had wanted to. But he felt it was important for them to reach this last landmark before day's end.

Atwood was a bustling town in the daytime. But at about a half-hour before midnight the streets were dark and empty. There were three saloons along the main street, and they were still open, but there wasn't much noise coming from inside. Sumner looked the town over as they rode through. He had been there before, but it had been some time ago. He reined up in front of a closed-down general store and looked over at Dulcie. She looked very tired.

'I'm sorry I had to push you today,' he told her. 'But barring trouble, you could be home tomorrow.'

She replied quietly. 'It's all right.'

'My idea is to ride on through, and make a camp up ahead a bit.'

She sighed. 'Wesley. We haven't had the slightest hint that Duke is behind us. Please. I don't want to sleep another night on the ground.'

Sumner leaned on his saddlehorn. 'I knew I was being too hard with you. But we'll be a little safer out on the trail.'

'I just want to lay my head on a pillow tonight. How much difference could it make in safety?'

He finally nodded, reluctantly. 'All right. But not at one of these main street hotels. I think there's a small one over a couple of blocks. An out-of-the-way place. We'll stop there.'

'Oh, thank you,' she said with relief.

They followed the next side street a short distance and found the hotel that Sumner remembered. It didn't have the look of the bigger, better ones on the main thoroughfare, but it was what Sumner wanted. They hitched up outside, and went in.

It was a very plain interior. No potted palms and carpets there. A short reception counter took up most of the area, and a lanky clerk looked half-asleep behind it. He looked up when they entered.

'Ah. Guests! May I help you, folks?'

'We want to stay the night,' Sumner told him.

'Of course. We have some nice rooms on the second floor. Now. You are Mr and Mrs—?'

'We're not married, for God's sake,' Sumner frowned.

'Oh. Sorry.'

'Register us as Mr and Mrs Jones,' Sumner said.

'But you said—'

Sumner gave him a look.

'Oh. I see. Yes, sir. Will that be two rooms then?'

'No,' Sumner said brusquely. 'One room.'

Dulcie looked over at him quickly.

'Ah,' the clerk said, with a grin.

Sumner was irritated with the whole procedure. 'Just give us a room,' he growled.

'Yes, sir. If you'll just sign the book there. Or make your mark.'

Sumner scrawled his signature.

'We have a boy that can bed and feed your mounts,' the fellow added.

'Fine,' Sumner said curtly. 'Tell him to bring my guns in.'

'Yes, sir. And here's your key.'

Then they were on their way up a narrow stairway to their room.

At that same moment, over on the main street, Latham and Sloan rode slowly along taking in the looks of the place. They stopped in front of a saloon called the Plains Oasis. Latham turned to his right-hand man.

'They're here. I can feel it in my bones, Ira. I'd bet money on it.'

'I hope to hell they are,' Sloan remarked in a tired monotone. 'Let's get ourselves a drink. My tongue is scraping my mouth.'

'I should check these hotels on the main drag before I do anything else.'

Sloan frowned at him. 'If they're here, Duke, they'll still be here tomorrow morning. And whether they're here or on up the trail, we'll have them in the first hour

139

or so of daylight.'

Latham thought that over. 'Hell, you're right. We can get us a bed at one of these hotels as we check it out, and then get us a good rest before morning. Then I'll check at the others. And the saloons just in case. But I know they're here somewhere, Ira. I'd bet money on it.'

'A good plan,' Sloan agreed quickly, relieved.

'I'll be up before dawn, and get at it,' Latham said to himself. 'I want to do it myself. I'll get you when I find them. And we'll make our plans. If they're out on the trail, we'll catch them quick out there. But they're here.'

'Fine. Now let's offer this saloon some patronage. I'm past ready.'

Latham nodded. 'We can do that.'

At their hotel, up in room 214, Sumner and Dulcie had just looked the place over with distaste. There was a bed, a straight chair, a table on a wall, and an easy chair with the cover peeling off. No wall decorations, no carpet on the hardwood floor.

'It beats being out in the weather,' Sumner commented drily.

'You just got us one room,' Dulcie said quietly, studying his face.

He nodded. 'Do you think I'd let you out of my sight now, when we're so close to getting this done? No, you stay with me. You're going to use the bed. I was going to go get my bedroll, but I think if I push these chairs together, I'll be fine. You'll sleep with all your clothes on. Just like on the trail.'

She was mildly disappointed. She didn't even know

what she was hoping for, but it wasn't this. 'I can remove my vest and blouse.'

'No, you can't,' he said firmly. 'I like you just the way you are.'

'If I remember right, you seemed to like me very well without them when you had just shot Weeks and I came down the stair in my underclothes.' She watched his face.

Sumner gave her an acid look. 'Well. You are something to look at, Dulcie. And that's the problem. No clothes come off tonight. When you get home, you can sleep any way you want.'

'In the summer, I won't wear anything.' Observing him closely again.

'Damn it, Dulcie. Just go to bed.'

'Do you really want to spend the whole night here alone with me, with me over there and you way over here?'

'Exactly. Now, you heard me. Let's get some sleep.'

She slumped. 'All right, Wesley. But I'll be thinking about you.'

She got on to the old iron bed and drew a sheet over her. Sumner settled on the chairs and tipped his Stetson over his face. Within an hour they were both asleep.

It was several hours later, just before dawn, when Sumner awoke from a wagon rumbling past outside. He hadn't even removed the Peacemaker. He looked beside his easy chair and was surprised to see Dulcie sitting on the floor there, her head on the arm rest, and asleep.

His face softened, and he touched her auburn hair and gently stroked it. She woke to the touch.

141

'Dulcie. What are you doing over here?'

She yawned and even that gave her a sensual look. 'I couldn't sleep. I was happier over here.'

He sighed. 'It's almost dawn. We ought to get ready to leave.'

He got out of the chair and stretched, and Dulcie rose to her feet. 'I can't believe I'll be home today,' she said.

'All being well, you will. Your daddy will be very happy.'

She didn't respond. They washed in a bowl at a dry sink, and Sumner put the Stetson on. 'I'm going to leave you briefly. I'll get the horses brought around, and make sure he has my long guns down there. Then I'll walk down to that close-by restaurant and bring us some coffee. Maybe a couple of biscuits. But I have to trust you to stay put.'

'I will,' she promised him. She looked beautiful in the burgeoning light from outside as the sun made its presence noticed.

'I'll be right back. Lock the door after me.'

Then he left the room.

Over on the main street, at a better hotel, Latham and Sloan were also just leaving their room.

'You go get our mounts and bring them out front here,' Latham was saying. 'Then pound on a couple saloon doors and see if you rouse anybody. They might give you something. I'll check at hotels. We'll find them. Then it will be over.' He paused. 'I'll meet you at that little restaurant down the street. And we'll put our heads together there.'

Sloan nodded. 'None of this should take long. Good luck.'

Then they separated outside. Sloan got their mounts and tried at a couple of saloons but got no response. Then he headed for the restaurant. Latham was frustrated at the main street hotels, but was referred over to the one where Dulcie waited for Sumner.

'Why, yes,' the desk clerk told him when asked. He was the same man who had registered them. 'A couple like that did check in last night. An obvious gunslinger, and a girl. Registered as husband and wife.'

'Are they still here?'

'Yes. But I'm bringing their mounts around just now. The gentleman said he'd be back shortly.'

'The girl is here alone?'

'For the moment, yes.'

It was tempting. Dulcie was there and vulnerable. But Sumner could be back at any moment. And if not, they would never get away without a confrontation. And maybe on his terms. No, he would get Sloan and they would make a plan against Sumner that was to their advantage.

What Latham could not know was that, at that very moment, Sloan had walked into the restaurant where Sumner had just ordered a pot of coffee to go.

Sumner was sitting at a table, waiting, when Sloan entered. They saw each other immediately, and Sloan froze just inside the entrance. The only other customers were a pair of ranchers sitting at a rear table.

'I'll be a sonofabitch,' Sloan muttered. 'You're

Sumner, ain't you?'

'And you're Ira Sloan,' Sumner said softly. He rose carefully from the table. 'Where's Latham?'

The waiter had emerged from the kitchen, and delivered two plates of food to the ranchers. But then he and the ranchers were watching Sloan and Sumner.

Sloan was thinking fast. He knew Sumner was good. He needed an advantage. 'He's here.'

'Really?' Sumner said, 'Where? Under a table?'

Sloan looked toward a rear door that led to the kitchen. 'He'll be here. And then you'll be boxed in, bounty man.'

'Well, then, we better get it over with,' Sumner said in a deadly voice, his gunhand hanging loosely beside the Peacemaker.

Sloan took a stance. But then he glanced behind Sumner, where the ranchers and waiter had quietly moved aside. 'Oh. You wanted Latham. Now you got him.'

Sumner didn't really believe the diversion, but he turned his head for just a half-second. And in that small moment, Sloan drew his Schofield .45 and fired.

Sumner, though, had heard the revolver slide from its holster, and had begun a drop into a half-crouch as Sloan fired. The Peacemaker answered fire in the next half-second, the guns making a roaring echo in the room. Sloan's shot, instead of striking Sumner mid-chest, hit him in the low neck, just missing the jugular. Sumner's lead smacked Ira Sloan just over the heart and sent him crashing loudly through a plate glass window directly behind him, hitting the narrow porch outside on his back.

The big Colt flashed in bright sunlight as it turned over into its resting place. Gunsmoke lofted to the tin ceiling. The three men at the rear rose from a crouched position. The waiter whistled between his teeth.

Sumner put his left hand to his neck and it came away stained red. But it felt like a shallow flesh wound. He threw a double eagle coin on to his table and glanced at the waiter. 'That's for the coffee and the window.'

Outside, he stopped a moment to look at Sloan. He was very dead, with a look of surprise still on his heavy face.

Worried about Dulcie now, Sumner hurried back towards their hotel. And just as he turned off the main street, Duke Latham turned on to it from a different side street, missing Sumner completely. He had walked just a half-block when he saw the small crowd gathered outside the restaurant. He stopped for a moment, a bad feeling in his stomach. Then he walked on up to the crowd and saw Sloan lying there with a man bending over him.

'Good God!' he muttered.

He didn't have to ask what had happened. They had found Sumner.

He swore several times under his breath, and went and leaned against the front of a store building.

His first thought was that he should have killed Dulcie while he had the chance. Now there was only him against Sumner. And Sumner had already demonstrated his deadliness by killing both of his men. Now, if he stayed in town, it would be Sumner hunting him.

His head whirled with wild thoughts. Maybe he could

145

wait for Sumner to come to him. Ambush him from cover and back-shoot him. But that could be very dangerous. Then he remembered the Remington rifle on his mount's irons, and got an even better idea. He was very good with the long gun, maybe better than Sumner.

He would ride out now, while Sumner was checking Dulcie out and maybe making a quick search for him. He would find a good spot out on the trail north, and wait for them. He would probably be able to take them both down before Sumner even knew where he was.

In the next ten minutes he got his horse at his hotel, rode past their hotel and saw that their mounts were still rail-hitched outside, and then rode on out of town.

Sumner had already found that Dulcie was still safe, and she had just discovered that he was wounded. She had given a little cry of alarm, and was now in the process of putting a makeshift bandana around his neck from a torn piece of pillowcase. He sat on the edge of the bed with Dulcie standing over him.

'It was Sloan that shot you?'

He nodded. 'He's dead.'

A small smile etched itself on to her face. 'Are you sure you're all right? We should have a doctor look at that.'

'We don't have time for that. Anyway, it's already healing. I should be out looking for Latham. But I'm afraid to leave you again.'

'Do you think he knows Sloan is dead?'

'Yes. I suspect they were meeting at the restaurant. But we don't know whether he's still here or has left.' He saw the curious look on her face.

146

'He might prefer to ambush us out on the trail rather than meeting me in a face-to-face. After finding Sloan.'

Her smile reappeared. 'They're all afraid of you, aren't they?'

Sumner gave her a sober look. 'Don't make me something I'm not, Dulcie. Any time I face down I can make a mistake. One that could be fatal.'

The smile faded away, but her confidence was not shaken. 'I don't think you make mistakes.'

He sighed, and got off the bed. He tied his blue bandana over the bandage. 'I could look for him all day here and not find him. But I have a feeling he isn't here. I reckon we could just ride out and hope he's not out there.'

'I'm sorry I talked you into stopping here,' she said quietly. 'I was sure they had given up on me.'

'No, this is better,' he said. 'This is bringing it all to a head, and under fairly favourable circumstances. On the trail, they might have killed us in our sleep. Come on, I'm not going to look for him. Let's ride out.'

Sumner was very cautious leaving the hotel, watching for Latham. But unknown to him, Latham was miles away, on the trail north.

Sumner hadn't brought the coffee back with him after the shoot-out with Sloan, so after they had ridden for just over an hour, they stopped briefly under a cottonwood and made a fire. They heated up some of their own coffee and ate some stale biscuits with it just for temporary sustenance. Dulcie was very quiet.

'Are you all right?' he finally asked her.

147

'This is my last day alone with you.'

'I've been thinking that myself.'

She looked very sober. 'These have been the best days of my life,' she said, looking at the ground.

Sumner regarded her seriously. 'Maybe you better withhold judgement on that till this last day is over.'

She threw the rest of her coffee on to the ground. 'I'm ready when you are,' she said abruptly, and went to her horse without looking at him.

They rode in silence for over an hour, with Sumner scanning the terrain ahead any time he saw a place where Latham could find cover for ambush. Finally they came to a place in the trail where a few low boulders encroached on the right side of the trail. And as they approached, Sumner thought he caught a glimpse of sun-flashed metal behind a head-high boulder about a hundred yards ahead. He held up his hand for Dulcie to stop, and reached down to slide his Winchester rifle from its saddle scabbard. And at that same moment, with his head and torso slightly bent forwards, a shot rang out from behind the boulder.

The lead would have hit him in centre chest, but because of his simultaneous movement with the shot, he was struck a grazing blow to the head that creased his scalp just above his right ear, and knocked his Stetson off.

Sumner felt a dizziness from the wound, and swore almost inaudibly. 'Dismount!' he yelled then at Dulcie. 'Hit the ground!'

Dulcie threw herself off her mount and crawled quickly towards a large clump of bushes a short distance away.

148

There were no boulders or other cover available near them. Halfway there another shot rang out and dug up dirt just beyond Dulcie's head. She gave a little cry, and then reached the questionable cover of the shrubbery.

Sumner had dismounted and the stallion had run off behind him. He went to one knee and returned fire to the boulder where the edge of a face showed. He fired again, chipping rock beside the shooter's head.

'He found us!' he called over to Dulcie. 'Stay put and do what I tell you!'

He knew her cover was marginal. Her mount had trotted off just a few yards and was rearing and whickering nervously. Another shot rang out and tore up shrubbery within inches of Dulcie's left arm.

A startled cry from her. 'Don't let him kill me, Wesley!' he heard her say.

'I won't,' he answered. Then he raised the rifle again and shot her horse in the head.

The animal snorted once and fell heavily to the ground not ten feet away, and in front of them. It was dead when it landed.

Sumner returned more fire to the boulder. 'Run and take cover behind your horse!' he yelled at her.

Dulcie was stunned by his extreme action. But she got to her knees, and then ran very low to the horse and fell behind its substantial corpse. A shot rang out and thumped into the animal's torso just above her. And in that instant Sumner ran to the horse and dived for cover beside her.

'You shot my horse!' she said breathlessly when he arrived.

149

'Would you rather it was a bullet in you?' he said, studying the boulder.

Suddenly Latham's shrill voice came from the boulder.

'Well done, Sumner! Just what I would have done! And now we play a little game! A game of life or death! And that Colt won't help you now! You have to go against my long gun! And I'm pretty good with it!'

'Talk is cheap, Latham! Let the rifle do your talking!' He raised up to take a look, and there was another echoing explosion and Sumner felt the lead buzz past his right ear. He swore again, ducking down.

'He's right. He's good with that.'

Dulcie's pretty face was clouded over with raw fear. When she spoke, her voice broke. 'Oh, Wesley. You're bleeding. Is it over for us?'

'Hell, no. And the blood is just a graze. Stay calm. Time is on his side. He'll flank us to get a better look. He has cover all the way to our right.'

'It's just a matter of time, Sumner!' Latham called out again. 'You're dead and don't know it! You, too, baby Provost!'

'Oh, God,' Dulcie mumbled.

Sumner grabbed her arm. 'Listen to me. I'm going to kill him. Do you believe me?'

She hesitated. 'Yes.'

'Now keep your head down. I'm going to make a run for those bushes you were behind. I'll have a better view from there. He'll take a shot at me. When I tell you to, scream! Scream loud!'

Dulcie frowned. 'All right.'

150

Sumner got his feet under him, and a moment later he was making a crouching run for the bushes, fifteen feet away. When he was almost there, a shot rang out and tore at his shirt, burning a short crease on his shoulder. He yelled out in mock pain as he hit the ground at the bushes.

'Scream,' he said quietly from his new cover.

Dulcie, staring towards him, let out a terrible scream as directed. Then there was complete silence from both positions. After a moment, Sumner hissed harshly to her. 'Tell him I'm dead. Yell at him.'

Dulcie nodded. 'Damn you, Duke! You killed him! You killed him!'

Sumner had slowly gotten to one knee behind his cover, and now aimed the Winchester at the edge of the boulder.

'Maybe!' Latham yelled. 'Maybe not!'

Dulcie, seeing Sumner ready, took a chance. She rose up to her full height. 'You bastard! Go ahead, shoot me! I don't care any more!'

In just a moment Latham's head emerged from behind the boulder, tentatively. 'You wouldn't lie to an old friend, would you, girl?'

Sumner took careful aim at the part of Latham's head he could see, and the Winchester roared out. At the boulder, hot lead struck Latham like a club on the bridge of his nose and sent splintered bone back through his brain pan. His head whiplashed, and then he was down.

'Did you . . . ?' from Dulcie.

'Yes,' Sumner said casually.

151

Dulcie let out a long breath. She was trembling. Sumner walked over to the boulder and looked down at Latham. The back of his head was blown away. His eyes were open, unseeing. When Sumner got back to Dulcie, she fell into his arms.

'It's over,' he told her. 'And you were wonderful. I couldn't have done it without you.'

She gave him a wry smile. 'I'll bet.'

'I'll go get the stallion, he's over by those trees. He missed all the excitement.' A half-grin. 'He can carry us both to the first town. We'll get you a replacement there. I think we can still make it back by day's end.'

She was still in his arms. She looked deep into his eyes. 'Whatever Papa is paying you, it isn't enough.'

He released her gently. 'If I'd known you before, he could have got me for nothing.'

That took her breath away for a moment, and she was silent.

'Now let's get you home,' he told her.

TEN

The big stallion was getting tired when Sumner and Dulcie reached the first town after taking up the trail again. Sumner stopped briefly at a doctor's house and medication was put on his scalp wound, and a real bandage on his neck. The shoulder wound was already caked over. They bought Dulcie a pinto pony that was a better ride for her than Weeks' mount, and then resumed their journey. There were no more stops, and they arrived at the Provost ranch in late afternoon.

When they crossed Wolf Creek on to Provost land, Dulcie asked Sumner to stop for a moment.

'This is where it happened,' she said, looking around her. 'This is where Duke surprised us.' She let out a long breath. 'That seems like a hundred years ago.'

'All those memories will fade,' he assured her.

She turned to him. 'Not the ones with you.'

He didn't respond. They rode on to the ranch house, and passed under a big gate into a wide yard.

There were a few ranch hands there, and they just stared with jaws dropped as the two riders passed them.

153

Corey Ross, the cowboy who had been with Dulcie when she was taken, but was not harmed by Latham, was chopping kindling right in their path.

'Oh, my God!' he gasped out.

Dulcie smiled. 'Hi, Corey.'

They rode on up to the house, where Jake Cahill was standing talking with another man. He glanced up at them distractedly, then took a second look. He frowned, as if he couldn't believe his eyes.

'Dulcie!' In a hushed undertone.

She gave him a lovely smile. 'Evening, Jake. I think you've met Wesley.'

Cahill got hold of himself, and rushed off the porch as the two dismounted. 'My God, I don't believe it! To tell you the truth, I'd given up on ever seeing you again!' He hugged Dulcie briefly, and then extended his hand to Sumner. 'You did it! Maynard kept telling me you would.'

Sumner smiled wearily. 'I'm glad he didn't lose faith. Sometimes I did myself.'

Cahill was grinning from ear to ear. He turned to stare at Dulcie again. 'I don't believe it. I really don't believe it!'

'It's good to see you again, Jake,' Dulcie told him.

'Oh, my God. Maynard. I think he's in his office. Wait till he sees you! Come on, let's go in.'

The three of them entered the coolness of the interior, with its rich look. Sumner saw Dulcie looking around, enjoying seeing everything again. Cahill arrived at Provost's office doorway ahead of them.

Provost was there, studying some papers. He heard Cahill approach, and looked up at him, standing in the doorway.

Provost frowned. 'Jake. What is it?'

Cahill took a deep breath in. 'Well. There's no easy way to tell you. Just don't have no heart attack on me now. Dulcie is back.'

And at that very moment, Dulcie appeared there, too, with Sumner just behind her.

Provost's face revealed the tumbling of several emotions as he rose slowly from his chair. 'Dulcie? Is it really you?'

'It's me, Papa. Thanks to Wesley here. I'm really back.' She ran to the desk he stood behind, and threw herself into his arms.

A stunned Provost accepted her awkwardly for a moment, then he was hugging her to him so tightly she could barely breathe.

'My girl! My baby.'

Tears were running down the cheeks of both of them. Sumner stood across the room, watching with pleasure. Cahill looked very emotional.

'I'll leave you three now,' he said quietly to Sumner. Then he was gone.

Provost had pulled his daughter away from him, at arm's length, so he could get a good look at her. 'Are you all right, honey? Did they hurt you?'

'Not really, Papa. I'm fine.'

Provost took her with him over to Sumner. 'I kept telling everybody. That you could do it.' He proffered his hand to Sumner, and Sumner took it.

'It's the best job I've ever taken,' Sumner told him honestly.

Dulcie smiled her lovely smile at him. 'Did you know how good he is, Papa?'

He returned her smile. 'I saw him shoot. That was enough for me.' He turned to Sumner. 'How did it go? Will we ever see Latham again?'

'Not unless you dig him up,' Sumner responded.

'Wesley got them all, Papa,' Dulcie added proudly. Her gaze fixed admiringly on Sumner.

Provost nodded his approval. 'Good. I'm very grateful, Sumner. You just rid the world of some especially ugly trash.'

'He was quite marvellous,' Dulcie said. 'I'll never see anything like it again.'

Provost was watching his daughter's face when she looked at Sumner. 'I reckon you think pretty highly of this fellow.' With a tentative grin.

Dulcie hesitated, took a breath in. 'Yes.'

There was a short silence in the room. Then Provost spoke again. 'Well. It looks like you and me have some business to conduct, Sumner.'

'Whenever you're ready,' Sumner told him.

'We can do it right now. I just have to get into my safe here.'

'I'll just go freshen up then,' Dulcie told them. 'You'll be staying the night, won't you, Wesley?'

Sumner shook his head. 'I have business elsewhere, Dulcie. I'll be moving on.'

She sighed heavily. 'I knew you'd say that.' With a light frown. 'I'll be back shortly.'

In the next few minutes, Provost got a wad of cash from his safe, counted it out, and handed it over to

Sumner in an over-size leather poke. 'That should keep you in grub for a spell.'

'Appreciate the business, Provost. It was very satisfying to me, too.'

'Are you sure you won't take that bonus I offered you when we started all this? I'd have given this ranch to get my girl back.'

'I couldn't,' Sumner said. 'It was a pleasure riding with her.' He paused. 'I know you know this. But you have a very special daughter there, Provost.'

Provost studied his face. 'I think she's a little sweet on you.'

Sumner was embarrassed. 'I got that figured out myself. I'm right sorry about that. I did nothing to encourage it.'

'I don't think you would,' Provost said. 'That's why you won't stay the night.'

'It doesn't seem appropriate.' He rose, with his poke. 'I'll be making tracks now. It was a pleasure knowing you and your daughter.'

They went outside together, and Cahill was waiting for them on the porch. 'All business settled?' Cahill asked.

'All done,' Sumner told him. 'Hope to see you around somewhere, Jake. Provost.'

Cahill clapped him on the shoulder. 'You were a Godsend,' he said quietly.

Just at that moment Dulcie came hurrying out on to the porch. Face slightly flushed. Auburn hair down long, vest gone, looking very feminine.

'You would have left without saying goodbye, wouldn't you?'

Sumner stared at her beauty. 'Of course not.' He put a hand on her shoulder. 'I'm going to miss you, Dulcie.' Then he walked out to the stallion at the hitching rail.

He shoved the leather poke into a saddlebag, and was about to mount, when Dulcie suddenly came running out to him and threw her arms around him and kissed him.

Sumner was caught off guard, but he let it happen. Holding her to him. Allowing himself to enjoy the moment, despite Provost's presence.

Her eyes were damp. 'I'll always love you,' she said quietly.

Her words carried to the porch, and Provost and Cahill exchanged a knowing look.

Sumner finally released her. Despite his instincts to the contrary, Dulcie had finally moved him over some invisible line. He studied her lovely face for a moment. 'Maybe you are a woman,' he said. 'You sure showed some maturity out there on the trail. And here.'

She gave him a smile that he felt inside him.

'Tell you what. I have a few wanted dodgers in my saddlebag that I want to follow up. But I've been thinking. Maybe a man can change who he is. Under the right circumstances.' He paused. 'Maybe I might just be ready to hang this Peacemaker on a wall in a year or so. And if you're so inclined, I could stop back past here to see if you're married yet.'

Dulcie couldn't believe what he had just told her. 'You mean it? You'd come back here? Just for me?'

'You'll be more grown then. Inside.'

'Oh, my God! I'll be here, Wesley. Waiting.'

158

Provost called to Sumner from the porch. 'You'll be welcome here any time you'd care to return!'

Sumner smiled at him. Giving Dulcie another long look, he mounted the stallion. In another moment he was riding out through the big gate, with several ranch hands waving him off.

When he was out of sight, Dulcie returned to the porch, her eyes still moist.

'Well, well,' Provost grinned at her.

She just kissed him on the cheek, and went inside to be by herself.

A short time later, at the Wolf Creek crossing, Sumner reined up and sat there for a moment, remembering. He and Dulcie had come through a harrowing adventure together. Those dangerous moments, and the way Dulcie had handled them, had put something between them. Something that had permanence to it. He spurred the stallion across the creek.

For the first time in his life, he decided, he owned an acceptable future for himself.

Some day soon he would take possession of it.